He sat there and watched her. It was no hardship, looking at Lili. Within minutes, her breathing evened out and she slept.

He thought how he really did need to be careful. It was one thing to find a way to get along with her.

And another altogether to let her get too close.

He'd found a certain balance. Letting her get too close could cast him into chaos. He couldn't afford that.

Still, he remained in the chair, watching her. Feeling strangely peaceful, almost daring to imagine what it could be, between them.

And then reminding himself that he was only going to learn to get along with her, to live in peace with her. They were never going to have the kind of marriage she dreamed of.

And he needed to remember that.

Dear Reader,

On a fateful morning in April, Princess Liliana, heir presumptive to the throne of Alagonia, surrendered her virginity to Prince Alexander of Montedoro, third-born of the Bravo-Calabretti princes. And wouldn't you know? Now she is pregnant.

Pregnant. By Alex, the bane of her childhood. Really. Alex is the last person she ever should have had sex with. She's still not sure what came over her. They've never gotten along. She thinks he's mean and self-absorbed. He thinks she's flighty and shallow. It's been that way for as long as either of them can remember.

Marriage between them will bring only disaster. But she is a princess. For her, the strictest rules apply. Everyone—including Alex—insists that she do the right thing and marry him.

All her life Lili has dreamed of true love, of a marriage of equals. She doesn't see how she'll ever have her dream with Alex. Especially now. Since his four years as a prisoner in Afghanistan, Alex is worse than ever. He hardly comes out of his rooms at the palace, except when he's training his elite corps of paramilitary operatives.

It's a good thing that Lili is a lot more patient and resourceful than many realize. Alex may be terrible husband material. But Lili refuses to be daunted. One way or another, she's got her sights set on love everlasting. And nothing, not even the impossible prince she *has* to marry, is going to stand in her way.

Happy reading, everyone,

Christine Rimmer

THE PRINCE SHE HAD TO MARRY

CHRISTINE RIMMER

HARLEQUIN®

entertain, enrich, inspire™

Recycling programs
for this product may
not exist in your area.

ISBN-13: 978-0-373-65703-2

THE PRINCE SHE HAD TO MARRY

www.Harlequin.com

Printed in U.S.A.

Books by Christine Rimmer

CHRISTINE RIMMER

came to her profession the long way around. Before settling down to write about the magic of romance, she'd been everything from an actress to a salesclerk to a waitress. Now that she's finally found work that suits her perfectly, she insists she never had a problem keeping a job—she was merely gaining "life experience" for her future as a novelist. Christine is grateful not only for the joy she finds in writing, but for what waits when the day's work is through: a man she loves who loves her right back, and the privilege of watching their children grow and change day to day. She lives with her family in Oregon. Visit Christine at www.christinerimmer.com.

For my mom,
who found her true love at fifteen.
I love you, Mom.
And we all miss you so much.

Chapter One

"Which of your sons has impregnated my virgin daughter?" King Leo demanded so loud that the words seemed to bounce off the damask-covered walls. He swept the room with a burning, accusatory glance.

Liliana, Princess of Alagonia and also the formerly virgin daughter in question, cringed at her spot near the tall, elegantly carved, gold-trimmed double doors. You could have heard the proverbial pin drop.

The Bravo-Calabretti family, surprised during their morning meal, did not say a word. They sat perfectly still in the beautiful antique chairs around the large pedestal table. They stared, unmoving, even the children—eyes tracking from Leo to Lili and then back to her furious father again.

They were all there, too, in the breakfast room of Her Sovereign Highness's private apartment at the Prince's Palace of Montedoro. Every one of them: HSH Adrienne and her prince consort, Evan, and their four sons and five daughters.

Also present were the heir apparent's two young children and the new wife and son of the second-born prince, Rule.

King Leo, his face red as the heart of Montedoran orange, started shouting again. "Who is the culprit? Who has dishonored my one and only child?"

Lili longed simply to sink through the inlaid marble floor, to crawl under the lush, blue-accented Savonnerie rug. Dear, sweet Lord in heaven. Did it get any worse than this? She was afraid it just might. She had tried her very best to keep her father from finding out about the baby—at least not until she'd had a chance to talk to the exasperating prince she'd made the terrible mistake of having sex with.

But she'd received no answer to the letter she'd sent him. He had not returned her two furtive calls. And before she could decide what her next move should be, her father had found out.

Lili was an only child and her father loved her absolutely. And somehow, he always knew when something was bothering her. He'd been after her for weeks to tell him what the matter was. He'd kept insisting that she was looking pale, that she never smiled anymore. She had repeatedly denied there was anything wrong.

And then, last night: disaster at dinner. It was the lamb that did it. Just the smell of it had her running from the table.

Her father had jumped up and come after her. He barreled into her apartment right behind her and even followed her all the way to the toilet, where he knelt on the floor beside her and held her head while she was repeatedly sick. He was beside himself with worry, certain she was desperately ill, that she must be knocking at death's door.

As soon as she finished ejecting the meager contents of her stomach, she had tried to soothe him, tried to reassure him that it was nothing. A little indigestion, a touch of the flu....

But he wouldn't be soothed. He questioned the servants. They loved her and were loyal to her, every one of them. They all tried to protect her, to claim they knew nothing. But they did know. The servants always do. And her father could be frightening, with his deep, commanding voice, his blustery manner and imaginative, if essentially baseless, threats.

In the end, a young chambermaid had broken down in tears and revealed the truth. "Sir, I'm so sorry, Sir. Her Highness is…with child."

At which point her father hit the ceiling. For half the night, he'd kept after Lili, demanding to know the name of the scurvy dog who had taken advantage of her. Lili refused to tell him.

And her father took action. He was positive it had to be one of the Bravo-Calabretti princes.

Unfortunately, he happened to be right—not that she'd admitted it. She hadn't. In fact, she had not so much as spoken a single word to His Majesty since well before midnight.

At two in the morning, he'd herded her aboard the royal jet. They took off for the airport at Nice. Alagonia was an island state off the coast of Spain. Montedoro, a short drive from Nice, claimed a particularly scenic slice of the glorious Côte d'Azur. The direct flight took just over five hours, which Lili had spent in her sleeping compartment with the door firmly shut against her father and his fulminating glances, his dire accusations and his never-ending insistence that she give him the name of the "low-born son of a dog" who had "used and abused" her. She'd tried to sleep but couldn't.

And now, as she trembled in her spot near the breakfast-room door, Lili tried desperately not to further disgrace herself—no! She would not be sick now. Not here, in front of her red-faced, wild-eyed father and all those staring Bravo-Calabretti princes.

And while she was busy not letting herself throw up, she also took great care not to look directly in the face of the one who'd relieved her of her virginity. The one who had refused to answer her letter or return her calls. Maybe now he would finally condescend to get in touch with her.

Even though she didn't dare meet his eyes for fear she would give him away, she silently prayed he would keep his mouth shut—for now. Let her father get nowhere with his histrionics. Eventually the king would wind down. Then she and the father of her child could discuss the situation in private, just the two of them, as they should have done long before now.

"I demand that the culprit stand and face me," her father blustered on. "I demand satisfaction and I demand it immediately!"

Yet more dead silence in the breakfast room.

And then, slowly, every Bravo-Calabretti head but the youngest ones swiveled in Prince Damien's direction. Lili wasn't particularly surprised. Damien was the family jet-setter, famous with the ladies. She knew what they all must be thinking: Who else could it be but Damien? Surely not Rule. Yes, Rule had been expected to propose to Lili for years, but they all knew he thought of her like a sister, that he'd never made any kind of advances toward her. And he was now happily married to the brilliant American, Sydney O'Shea, whom Lili truly admired.

Well, and it *hadn't* been Rule. It wasn't Damien either. But only two people in the room knew that.

King Leo didn't miss the way everyone glanced in Damien's direction. "Aha," he crowed hotly. "So, then. It's *you,* Damien. I suspected it might be. Stand," he commanded, whipping out the ceremonial scimitar he'd strapped on when they'd left the royal jet. How utterly mortifying. Leave it to her father to bring a scimitar. He swung the blade back and forth. It sang through the air of the too-quiet room. And then he assumed a fighting stance, the long, curving sword held high. "Stand and face me, you offal-eating swine."

Beyond humiliated now, Lili stifled a moan of pure misery. Her father was a fair man and a good ruler—except when his fury was roused. "Papa," she pleaded, "I beg you. This is not about you. This is between me and the father of my child. I want you to stop this. Now."

Her father ignored her.

Damien started to stand. Leo lunged forward and Lili opened her mouth to admit that Damien was not the man.

But before she made a sound, Damien's twin, Alexander, pushed back his chair and rose. "Sir, you have it wrong. Damien is innocent. I am the guilty one." Alex stood tall, his powerful shoulders drawn back, his haunted eyes level, frighteningly blank.

Lili clapped her hand over her mouth and swallowed bile. Yes, she understood that Alex had no choice but to reveal himself at that point. He couldn't just sit there and allow her father to take his ridiculous scimitar to poor Damian, who for once was *not* guilty of seducing someone he shouldn't have.

But still…dear Holy Virgin, what now?

Everyone was gaping in shock.

They couldn't believe that Alex was the one, which didn't surprise Lili. She could hardly believe it herself—and she'd been there when it happened. They all knew that she'd always despised Alex, *and* that he felt the same way about her. Plus, well, Alex wasn't interested in women anyway. Not even in women he liked and respected. Not anymore. Not since whatever unspeakable horrors had befallen him in Afghanistan.

And yet…

The two of them did have sex together. Just once, in the second week of April. Once. That was all it had taken to plant a new life inside her, to change her world forever.

Alex. She'd lost her virginity to Alex. She still had trouble believing she'd done that. Because, honestly, how *could* she?

Her father seemed as shocked as the rest of them. "Alexander?" he asked, his voice suddenly without force, utterly disbelieving.

But then his fury returned full force. With a bloodcurdling shout, he raised his sword again and went for Alex—Alex, who didn't so much as flinch, but simply stood there, apparently ready to take whatever punishment her father saw fit to inflict upon him.

"Stop!" Lili shouted.

Her father didn't even break stride. She rushed forward to intercept him.

But Her Sovereign Highness Adrienne, Lili's dear friend and Alex's mother, was faster.

Montedoro's monarch rose lightly to her feet. She had a truly calm, almost-pleased expression on her legendary face. As though she couldn't have been more delighted to learn that her dark and damaged son had actually lurched back to life long enough to impregnate Lili, whom everyone knew was like another daughter to her.

Adrienne planted her noble person between the enraged king and her third-born son. Her smile turned even sweeter as she faced down Lili's father. "Leo," she said gently in warm, melodious tones. "I'm so glad you've come. And I think that now would be the perfect opportunity to discuss the wedding, don't you?"

Chapter Two

There were top secret meetings all that day. Alexander had work he should have been doing. But he put his work aside to be there while negotiations for his marriage to Lili were carried through.

No, there was no question as to the marriage itself. There would be one, and right away. Within the next day or two, everyone agreed—that is, everyone except Lili.

But no one was listening to Lili. They all tuned her out, even though she babbled incessantly. About love. And relationships. And her rights as a twenty-first-century woman.

"This is between Alexander and me," she insisted. And, "I refuse to marry a man who doesn't love me." And, "I just think it's wrong, that's all. I just don't think it's right and I don't see how you all can carry on blithely making your plans when I have said over and over that this is *my* decision—mine and Alex's—and we need to be left alone to work this out, just the two of us. We need to come to some sort of *peace* between us, some sort of real understanding as people, as a woman and a man, before we can even begin to discuss something as enormous and life-altering as holy matrimony...."

They let her babble. They all knew you couldn't shut her up if you tried.

More than once, she'd turned those huge aquamarine eyes his way. She reproached him. "Alex. Please. You know we *have* to talk."

Whenever she turned those eyes on him, he only stared back at her long and steadily and without expression, until she gave in and looked away. Occasionally, Alex's mother would pat Lili's hand or give her a hug. And then the rest of them would go back to deciding what needed to be done.

Alex kept his peace through each of the interminable meetings. He sat at the bargaining table or stood by the door. And other than to make it perfectly clear that of course he and Lili would wed, he said nothing.

What *could* he say? He was still reeling in shock to learn that Silly Lili, as he always used to call her when they were younger, was carrying his child. He should have read her damned letter, or answered one of her strange, frantic telephone calls. But he hadn't read the letter. And when she called, she'd mentioned nothing about a pregnancy. He'd assumed she was just being emotional as usual, that she was only after an opportunity to exercise the unpleasant flair for the dramatic that she'd inherited from Leo. He'd been sure she only wanted a chance to cry and carry on, to call him a cad and a defiler of innocent women.

How could he have touched her? He was completely disgusted with himself at what he had done. He *wasn't* a defiler of innocent women.

Or he hadn't been. Until that day two months before, when he'd heard someone sobbing outside his palace apartment. He still had no idea what had possessed him to look and see who it was.

He'd opened his door and stuck his head out. And there was Lili, all in white, kneeling on the inlaid tiles of the corridor floor, her long, pale gold hair falling forward, hiding her pretty face, her slim shoulders shaking with her sobs.

She must have heard the door open because she glanced up. Still sobbing, her eyes red and her perfect nose redder, tears streaming down her cheeks, she caught sight of him in the doorway. With a cry of sheer misery, she leaped to her feet. "Oh, Alex. The most terrible thing has happened. It's Rule." She said his older brother's name with another agonized cry. "He's married someone else."

He should have retreated right then. He should have shut the door and locked it and not opened it again.

Instead, he'd pulled the door open wider. She must have taken that as an invitation. She'd thrown herself into his arms and drenched the front of his shirt with her tears.

By that point, he absolutely should have pushed her away and shut the door. But he hadn't. He'd taken her into his sitting room and sat with her on the sofa and listened as she continued wildly sobbing, as she poured out her misery—that his brother loved another, that Rule would never be marrying her now, that Rule didn't love her and never had. That she was nothing more than an honorary little sister to him, and always had been.

When she finally paused to suck in a few shaky, hiccupy breaths, he'd handed her a tissue and told her exactly what he was thinking. "Calm yourself, Lili. There is so much *true* suffering that exists in this world. Don't you realize how little your petty problems matter in the larger scheme of things?"

His remarks had not gone over well. Lili had responded in her usual way. With an ear-flaying shriek of outrage, she'd drawn back her hand to slap his face.

He should have let her do that, allowed her to vent a little more of her considerable frustration. But no. He'd automatically caught her wrist before she could carry through.

And that was when it happened.

He still had no idea how. Or why.

All at once, she was in his arms. She smelled like her name, like some fine, sweet, exotic flower. She…overwhelmed him. There was no other word for it. Silly Lili overwhelmed him. Somehow, at that moment, having her in his arms was like holding hope and light and all the good things that were lost to him forever. Her skin was so soft and her eyes were the incomparable blue of lapis lazuli.

And then her mouth was under his, opening, sighing….

Something snapped in him. Something gave way.

What happened then was raw and perfect and really quite beautiful.

With Lili.

Lili, of all people.

Afterward, she smiled. So softly. Contentedly. And she reached up and laid her delicate, graceful little hand against his cheek. "Alex," she whispered, as though his very name held wonder for her now.

He couldn't bear that. He didn't need her looking at him like that. She should never ever look at him like that.

And so he'd said without inflection, "You should go now."

She did go. She pulled on her clothes swiftly—and silently, for once. Without looking at him again, without so much as another word, she left him.

After she was gone, he'd called himself any number of ugly and richly deserved names. And then he'd told himself it was best for her if they simply put the unfortunate incident behind them, if they went on with their separate lives as though it had never happened.

That was what he'd been trying to do. And then she sent

that letter that he hadn't allowed himself to open. She'd called him. Twice. Both times she'd left messages demanding he call her but giving no reason whatsoever why he should.

Now, at last, he knew why. Now it all made sense.

There would be a child and that meant they *couldn't* put what had happened behind them. Now they only needed to do the right thing. And both her father and his family were as eager as Alex was to turn this potential disaster around.

A marriage between Leo's only daughter and one of the Bravo-Calabretti princes would bolster the sometimes-strained relations between Alagonia and Montedoro. For years, most of the world had assumed that Lili would end up wed to Rule. But Rule's heart had turned elsewhere. And none of the other three Bravo-Calabretti princes had seemed suitable matches for the Alagonian heir presumptive.

The baby, however, changed everything. Diplomatically speaking, Alex would do just as well as Lili's groom as his older brother would have. The marriage would not only give his unborn child his name, but it would also forge an important bond between his and Lili's countries.

No, he and Lili didn't care much for each other. Nonetheless, their union would be a useful thing in more ways than one.

At four that afternoon, in the sitting room of the sovereign's apartment, with all the doors firmly locked against spying eyes and listening ears, Lili was still arguing, still trying to put the brakes on. "Why should I marry Alex? How many times do I have to say it? He doesn't love me and I don't love him. We don't even *like* each other. And we're only asking for disaster to race to the altar this way."

Leo sent her one of his fulminating glances—but at least when he answered her, he wasn't shouting. "He's the father of your child, Liliana. You are two months along. There is no time to waste and you have no choice."

Lili sucked in an outraged breath—and started in again. "No choice? Excuse me. Of course I have a choice. This is not the dark ages, thank you very much, Papa. Nowadays, even a princess has a right to—"

"Shh, now, Lili. Hush." Alex's mother patted her hand. "It will be all right, my dearest. You'll see."

"But, Adrienne…"

His mother touched Lili's cheek. "Shh. Think." Gently she reminded Lili of what they all knew. "This could turn into an international incident. And no one wants that. I know it's hopelessly stuffy and backward in many ways, but the rules for you, Lili—the rules for all of us—are different. We're held to a higher standard. And neither your father nor Alex's father nor I want our names or our family reputations dragged through the mud. No one wants a child of yours and Alexander's to be born a bastard. Come now, Lili. You don't want your child to be illegitimate, do you? Your child, by rights, will rule Alagonia one day. Why make it possible for anyone to question those rights?"

"I, well, I…" Lili's full lower lip began to quiver.

His mother held out her arms. Lili went into them.

Adrienne held Lili close and stroked her slim back and said quietly to the rest of them, "So, then, the plan is made. As far as the world is concerned, Lili and Alex have been secretly in love for some time now—and are *already* married. That should serve to eliminate any potential for unpleasant public speculation as to the legitimacy of the child."

They all nodded agreement. Lili released a small, strangled sob, but for once didn't argue.

The story would be that he and Lili had just that day informed their families of their earlier elopement. Alex would shoulder the blame for the lack of a large, formal public ceremony. The official line would be that Alexander, such a private person after the horrible events he'd endured in Afghanistan, couldn't bear all the pomp and circumstance of a royal wedding. So they had exchanged their vows in private before a sympathetic and discreet priest.

They would tell the world that both families were stunned at the news. And also deliriously happy for the newlyweds. Love was what mattered after all. They were all beside themselves with joy to learn that Her Royal Highness Liliana and His Serene Highness Alexander had bound themselves to each other, heart and hand, for as long as they both should live.

The real marriage was to take place in secret the next day, as the world at large got the fabricated story that he and Lili had eloped more than two months ago.

Bound. To Lili. She would drown him in her endless tears. And if he managed to survive the flood, she would then proceed to talk him to death.

But it couldn't be helped and he knew it. For him and Lili, marriage was the only solution to this particular problem. And eventually, she would grow tired of trying to batter down a door he was never going to open. She would leave him alone to pursue his goals in peace. She would take care of the child and prepare herself—or their son, should the child be a boy—to rule Alagonia in time.

Once the plan was set, a light meal was brought in. They filled their grumbling stomachs as they waited for the lawyers to produce the endless array of necessary documents. When the documents were finally ready, they signed.

At last, at a little past nine, the final *i* was dotted. They were finished for the day.

Alex retired to his apartment. He showered and got into bed. To try and wind down a little, he treated himself to a few chapters of an excellent book on the covert operations of the special tactics units of the United States.

By one in the morning, he'd finished the book. The winding down was not happening. So he threw on some workout clothes and went to join the men of the all-new Montedoran special forces, which he had been instrumental in creating. The Covert Command Unit had barracks and training yards accessible through a series of tunnels beneath the palace.

Late into the night, Lili tossed and turned.

She'd been coerced. Unfair pressure had been brought to bear upon her. No one, not even Adrienne, whom she adored, had listened to her. In the States, they had a word for the way she'd been treated.

Railroaded.

Yes, she'd been railroaded into agreeing to marry a man she didn't like, a man who made no secret of the fact that he thought she was a useless, silly person who talked too much. She yearned to find a way to back out of the marriage tomorrow.

But there *was* no way. There was no escape for her. She was a princess, the heir to a throne, and as Adrienne had made so painfully clear, different rules applied for her. Her duty demanded that she put aside her own feelings and desires and marry Alex. And for the sake of her child and her country, she would do exactly that.

All her life, she had dreamed of true, forever love. She wouldn't have that now. Not with Alex. Alex didn't love her. He didn't love anyone. Maybe he *couldn't* love anyone. Not anymore, at any rate.

He'd always been a cool and distant sort of man. But since he'd been captured and held prisoner in Afghanistan, his cool nature had turned to ice. And the distance he'd always maintained between himself and others had become a chasm too wide and deep for anyone, even the most determined of women, to cross.

Lili shivered at the thought of a lifetime bound to him,

shackled to a man who never smiled, who looked right through her. The best she was ever going to get from Alex was the occasional bout of really splendid lovemaking.

Because that, at least, had been glorious. It seemed impossible that it could have been that good.

But it was—and she had been a virgin, untried and inexperienced, completely unskilled in the ways of passion and sexual fulfillment.

She sighed in spite of everything. It was a dreamy sigh. She couldn't help it. Alex had shown her heaven that day in April. He'd shown her heaven—and then coldly cast her out.

And what about the baby? Was there any hope for her child? Would her poor little one have to grow up with a distant, coldhearted father? Her own father was far from perfect, but blustery King Leo's unconditional love for her was the cornerstone of Lili's life. She didn't think she could have survived losing her dear mum five years ago if she hadn't had her darling papa to turn to during that bleak time.

No, she simply couldn't do it. International incident be damned, she would not let her child grow up with a distant, detached father.

Lili turned her head on the pillow and stared at the ornate miniature table clock by the bed. It was 3:02 a.m. And no matter what her father and Adrienne did or said, she was not going to be Alex's bride that day. Not unless she and Alex could first come to some basic agreement about the marriage they were entering into and the kind of life they were going to share.

She rose from the bed, slipped her feet into satin slippers and pulled on her blush-pink silk dressing gown. Before she could let herself weaken, before she gave up without even trying and returned to her bed, she hurried through the sitting room of the apartment that had always been considered hers when she visited the Prince's Palace.

Silently, she emerged into the corridor outside her rooms. She closed her door with great care. Then she took off at a run down the wide, arching hallways, her soft slippers making no sound on the marble floors.

Fortune smiled upon her, at least a little. She saw no one, which meant that no one waylaid her, no one asked her what in the world she thought she was doing, wandering the palace hallways so very late at night.

When she reached the door to Alex's suite, her courage failed her. She stiffened her spine and retied the sash of her robe and gave the beautifully carved door three sharp raps with her knuckles.

Nothing. No answer.

She knocked again. And then, pausing to send furtive glances down the hallway in both directions, she knocked a third time. She pressed her ear to the heavy door.

Not a sound within. He wasn't there.

Or, more likely knowing him, he *was* there, but he wasn't answering.

Hah. If he thought she could be put off so easily, he should prepare for a surprise. Lili had a hairpin and she knew how to use it. In fact, she thought as she stuck the two pin ends in the keyhole and twisted them in a manner both precise and effective, she was a lot more capable than many gave her credit for.

The simple lock turned and the door swung silently inward. For the first time in too long, Lili allowed herself a small smile of satisfaction.

The high-ceilinged antechamber, dimly lit by wall fixtures, was deserted. Lili tiptoed inside and silently closed and locked the door behind her.

"Alex?" she whispered. "Are you there?" And then she drew back her shoulders and tried again, louder. "Alex, I mean it. We have to talk." She waited. "Alex? Alex!"

Nothing.

She straightened her robe and flipped her hair back over her shoulders with both hands and marched into the dim sitting room. "Alex?"

No one was there.

So she turned to the hallway that led to his bedroom. When she got there, the door was shut.

As if a closed door could stop her now. She grasped the latch. Unlocked. She pushed the big door inward upon the darkened room—the room where Alex had carried her that bright April morning, the room where he had…

No. She wasn't going to think about it. She wasn't going to remember. She had more important things on her mind right now than the wonder and beauty that had occurred in this room—and the cold, heartless way he'd dismissed her afterward.

"Alex…"

Only silence greeted her. She flipped the wall switch and stared at the wide, empty, unmade bed. The tangled sheets and covers spilled to the floor. Apparently, Alex had not been able to sleep, either.

But where was he now?

The door to the bath stood wide. She marched over there and looked in.

No one.

Lovely. She'd worked up her courage to confront him, even gone so far as to break into his apartment. And he didn't even have the good grace to be here so that she could tell him exactly what she thought of him.

What now?

Suddenly, she felt like a balloon with a slow leak. She returned to the massive carved bed and hoisted herself up onto it. "Oh, Alex…" She blew out a discouraged breath and let her shoulders slump. "What *am* I going to do with you?"

She stared down at her little satin slippers and wondered if he would be back soon.

You just never knew with Alex. You could never predict the choices he might make. It was very annoying.

With another long sigh, she let her gaze wander. The room was large and well-appointed. Her glance caught on the night-table photo of Alex and that American friend of his—the one who had been with him in Afghanistan when he was captured, the one who had not made it back. In the photo, Alex and his friend sat together in a dusty open Jeep. They both wore desert fatigues and carried rifles.

They were also both grinning, the sunlight refracting off the lenses of their aviator sunglasses. Lili stared at Alex's image and wondered if she'd ever seen him grin like that. Judging by the square, flat-topped buildings in the background and the desert terrain, she guessed the picture must have been taken during that ill-fated trip to Afghanistan. Taken before either Alex or his friend had any idea what was going to happen to them.

She didn't know the details of Alex's capture and imprisonment. But she did know it had lasted four years. Four endless years during which he must have suffered terribly, during which his friend had lost his life. Four years until, somehow, six months ago, he'd managed to escape.

Lili flopped back onto the tangled sheets and stared up at the coffered ceiling. All right, she felt a tiny bit…abashed. Looking at that picture reminded her that Alex did have his reasons for being Prince Cold, Mean and Unresponsive. She couldn't even begin to imagine what he must have endured during his time as a prisoner. She needed to be more understanding, to keep in mind what he'd been through when she wanted to call him unflattering names and slap his expressionless face.

Lili kicked off her slippers. They plopped to the bedside

rug. She promised herself that she *would* try to be nicer to him. She *would* keep in mind the awfulness of what he'd survived. From this moment on, she'd make more of an effort to be understanding and patient and not to burst into tears or let her temper get the better of her.

She was so busy telling herself that she would really try and treat Alex more kindly that she didn't hear the outer door open or even notice that a light in the sitting room had popped on. She remained stretched across the tousled sheets on her back, her arms spread wide and her bare feet dangling over the side.

The last thing she expected was to hear Alex say, "Lili, it's almost four in the morning. What in hell are you doing here?"

She popped to a sitting position with a shocked little squeak. "Eek! Alex, you *scared* me."

He was dressed in a sweat-drenched T-shirt with the sleeves ripped off and a similarly sweaty pair of frayed gray sweatpants. In fact, everything about him was sweaty—his more-granitelike-than-ever face, his close-cropped, thick brown hair, his muscular arms and deep, broad chest.

There were scars on his arms and on his neck, pinkish-white and rough against his tanned skin. She started to feel real sympathy for him.

And then he muttered darkly, "I'll do a lot more than just scare you if you don't tell me why you're in my rooms."

Softly, she reminded him, "You wouldn't talk with me yesterday."

"That's because there was nothing to say."

I am not going to start shrieking at him. I am not going to slap his smug, cold face, she reminded herself. *He has suffered too much and I am going to be understanding and gentle with him.*

Lili straightened her robe, which had fallen open to expose a lot more of her thighs than he needed to see at that moment.

And she tried to look dignified, even if he had caught her sprawled in complete dishabille across his bed. "I've come to you stealthily in the middle of the night because I saw no other choice in the matter."

"No other choice," he echoed in a growl. "*I'll* give you another choice. Return to your rooms. Do it now."

No shrieking, she reminded herself again. And then she drew in a slow breath and hitched her chin higher. "Alex, I mean it. We really must talk."

Alex was certain he'd locked the outer door when he left. It wasn't a high-security lock, but it certainly should have served to keep Silly Lili out. "How did you get in here?"

She granted him a coy look from under her astonishingly long, silky eyelashes. "I have my ways."

It was no answer, but he realized about then that he probably wouldn't get an answer from her. The main thing was to get her to go. "Back to your rooms, Lili."

She sat even taller. "Not until we talk."

How many times did he have to remind her that they had nothing to say to each other? He started toward her, determined to get rid of her.

She put up a hand. "If you touch me right now, I am going to start screaming. I will scream as I run out your door and down the corridor, without even pausing to put on my slippers. I will wake up every servant and guest in the palace. It will not be pretty and everyone will blame you for abusing an innocent barefoot princess who happens to be dressed only in her nightclothes. And, of course, someone will leak the story to the tabloids, which will wreak havoc on all your carefully engineered plans to make it look as though you and I are passionately and totally in love."

He paused in midstep. "They are not my plans."

"Oh, I beg your pardon. You fully agreed to them." She

folded her arms under her beautiful, perfect breasts, causing the pink silk of her robe to cling more tightly. Now he could see the faint outline of her nipples. They were very fine nipples, as he remembered all too well.

He reminded himself that he needed to get rid of her. "We had no choice but to agree to those plans. I saw no other option, given our situation. And now, if you'll just go back to your—"

She cut him off. "We do have choices," she said in a so-noble tone that made his teeth hurt. "We *always* have choices."

"You are not only hopelessly naive, Lili, but you are also thoughtless and self-centered. And wrong."

Those enormous blue eyes glittered like sapphires— dangerous sapphires. "Insult me to your heart's content. It won't work. I'm not leaving until you *talk* with me."

"Lili," he said, rough and low. He dared another step.

She threw out a hand, palm out. "I mean it. I will scream."

He held her gleaming gaze with his own, steady on. "You wouldn't dare."

She smiled pleasantly—and stared right back. "Go ahead, try me."

He realized he was actually afraid she just might do what she'd threatened. She had him by the short hairs, damn those eyes.

Without another word, he turned on his heel and headed for the bath. Once through the door, he shut it. Rather harder than necessary. He twisted the privacy lock—even though, apparently, privacy locks were no good against her. Too bad. She would enter the bath at her own risk. He stripped off his sweat-drenched clothing and took a shower. A long shower.

When he finished, he put on the robe that hung on the peg behind the door and returned to the bedroom.

She was still there, sitting in the same spot on the bed,

her little hands folded in her lap. "I do hope your shower has refreshed you—and possibly even improved your attitude." She gave a shrug and a sigh. "Well. One can hope."

He said nothing to her, only exited back into the sitting room, where he proceeded directly to the liquor cabinet. He grabbed a crystal glass and a decanter of very old scotch and poured himself a stiff one. He was sipping it slowly when she spoke from behind him.

"We have more than my country and your country to think of, Alex."

He turned and faced her. She looked way too determined. And way too beautiful, with those amazing eyes of hers, those full pink lips and all that thick, silky, pale yellow hair. Raising his glass to her, he took another slow sip.

She laid her hand against her still-flat belly. "There's the baby. The baby is what matters most of all."

"Good. Then don't allow him to be born a bastard."

"Being born illegitimate is not the worst thing that can happen to a child."

"Of course it's not. But I wouldn't call it a *good* thing. Would you call it a good thing, Lili?"

"I didn't say it was a good thing."

He topped off his drink. "Because it's *not* a good thing. Not for a child who should have the right to a crown and could be denied that right because his mother refuses to marry his father."

"My baby will have a father who loves him—or her," she announced. "If you can't love this baby, the baby is better off without you."

"All right. I will love the baby." He set down the decanter. "Happy now?"

"Not especially. Alex, if you can't at least try to make a real marriage with me, I won't marry you." She spoke more softly then, and her eyes seemed suddenly far away. "All my life, I've wanted one thing above all—to have true love like my parents had. Like *your* mother and father have. Like Max had with Sophia." Maximilian was the heir to his mother's throne. Max's wife, Sophia, had died while he was in Afghanistan. "Love like Rule and Sydney have found."

He studied her for a long time. He pondered the goal: to get her to let him give their child his name. To achieve the goal, he should tell her whatever she needed to hear, which apparently was that he loved her. Deeply and completely. Somehow, he couldn't wrap his mouth around a lie that large. "I can't give you what you want, Lili. It's simply not in me." He steeled himself for her tears, for one of her big, emotional displays.

Her eyes remained dry. And when she spoke, it was calmly. Reasonably. "I realize that. I can accept that."

Did he believe her? Hardly. She might be the most annoying woman he'd ever known, the most overwrought and emotional, the biggest chatterbox. But within her there lurked a will of iron. If she wanted something strongly enough, she would never rest until she had it.

Or until she drove anyone who stood in the way of her having it stark, raving mad.

Plus, beneath all the sweetness and meaningless chatter, she was quite intelligent. Sometimes she behaved stupidly, but there was a perfectly good brain inside that gorgeous head of hers. She was using it now. He could see the cogs turning. She was about to lay down terms.

He already knew what kind of terms. Terms that would have him agreeing to give her more than he could afford to give, more than he even knew *how* to give anymore. Five years ago, maybe. But not anymore. Whatever that place was inside a man, that place a woman filled and made warm and good and hopeful. That place was dead in him now. Uninhabitable.

She went on. "What I want from you is for you to try."

He purposely did not make the scoffing sound that rose in his throat. "Try."

"Yes. I want you make an effort to be a real husband to me. I want you to spend time with me. I want you to have breakfast with me every day and dinner as well. I want you to give me—to give *us*—the evenings, that time *after* dinner. I want us to spend our evenings together, just the two of us. I want you to tell me about your day and I will tell you about mine. I want us to share, Alex."

Share. Did it get any worse? She wanted him to *share*.

She was still talking. "I want you to read the books I choose for you."

"Books. Hold on just a minute. You're choosing what books I read?"

"Not *all* the books you read, of course not."

"I suppose you'll have me studying those romance novels you so enjoy."

"Don't judge romance novels until you've read a few of them. One can learn a lot about love and life and relationships from a good romance."

He had no words to reply to that one. So he said nothing. He didn't really need to say much around Lili anyway. She had the talking covered, and then some.

She said, "No. Actually, I didn't plan to have you reading romances, though I'm sure it would be good for you if you did."

He made a grunting sound and left it at that.

"But I do think if you would just spend a little time with a few books on how to develop a meaningful and loving relationship with your spouse, it would really help you. Help *us*. And then once you've read the books I choose for you, we can discuss them—and tell me, have you been seeing a counselor or a priest?"

"For what?"

"For…help, with all you've been through. Surely you've noticed that you've changed, Alex."

"Yes, Lili, I've noticed. And no, I haven't seen a counselor or a priest and I don't intend to."

"Oh, Alex…"

"And as to those books on love and marriage that you mentioned…"

"Yes?"

He knocked back more scotch. "No."

Gingerly, she inquired, "No as to…"

All of it, he thought. He said, "Not the books, Lili. Or the priest. Or the counselor."

"Ahem. Well. What about the rest?"

He saw no other way. He was going to have to pretend to go along, to bargain and then reluctantly come to an agreement. He needed to convince her that he would do what she wanted, that he would *try.* "Yes to the meals—the breakfasts, the dinners."

"And the evenings? What about the evenings?"

He let the silence draw out before grunting, "All right, damn it. The evenings, too."

She actually clapped her hands and the most radiant smile bloomed on those plump, way-too-kissable lips. "Oh, I'm so glad."

"But not *every* evening," he said. "Two evenings a week."

"Six."

"Three."

"Four."

He repeated his previous offer. "Three."

She considered, then stipulated, "Friday, Saturday and Sunday."

"When possible."

"Three at any rate. And you have to try to make them the evenings I just asked for."

There was that word again. *Try.* Such a flexible word. And such a simple thing, to say one was trying when one actually wasn't. "All right," he grudgingly agreed.

"Wonderful. And we will share an apartment—this apartment will be fine." She was too damn quick by half. He'd been counting on them keeping their separate suites, on her heading back to Alagonia as soon as the ink was dry on their secret marriage license.

But he supposed there was no help for it. If they were to pretend to be deeply in love for the whole world to see, they certainly couldn't be living in separate quarters. "Fair enough."

"And I will expect you to be my birth coach when the baby arrives. That means we'll be going to childbirth classes together."

He sent her a speaking look, one that told her exactly what he thought of being her birth coach.

Quickly, she added, "Spare me the put-upon glances. You'll have time to become accustomed to the idea of the childbirth classes. They won't even begin for four or five months yet."

Anything could happen in four months. And the goal was to get her to marry him tomorrow. "All right."

"Wonderful, then. For the first year, I'm willing to live here, in Montedoro, with you."

The first *year?* "How generous of you."

She nodded. "I know you have your…secret fighting force that you're, um, working with."

"The CCU is not a secret, Lili," he informed her flatly. "Montedoro has no standing army. It's simply expedient for us to have a small, specially trained corps of men at the ready to take action in a critical situation."

"Yes. Expedient." She wore an irritatingly patient expression. "I understand. And as I was saying, you need to be here for that. And as I mentioned earlier, I know you've been through a lot."

"What does what I've 'been through' have to do with anything?" he demanded.

She answered carefully. "I just meant you've only been back for six months. I think you need more time here, in Montedoro, at the only home you've ever known, more time to…heal."

To heal? How so? His wounds no longer festered. He'd put back on the thirty kilos he'd lost during his captivity, and then some. His "healing," such as it was, was done. But he didn't say that. He said nothing.

And she continued, "I've always loved Montedoro anyway. So let's say a year, together, here at the Prince's Palace. I'll clear my calendar."

"For the entire year?" She was constantly giving speeches at charity functions, working diligently to establish trusts for the needy. "Isn't a year a bit extreme?"

"Perhaps, but necessary. I want our marriage to work. There's the baby to think of, anyway. I'll want to take it easy from seven months or so on. And then I'll need a few months to concentrate on our newborn. After the year is up, though, we will discuss a move to Alagonia—or a way to divide our time between our two countries."

He had to give her credit. She was quite the negotiator. But it didn't matter what he agreed to now. She would be fed up with him long before a year had passed. In the end, she would be only too happy for them to lead separate lives. He would make sure of that. "Agreed," he said.

She folded her hands in front of her. "I want us to be happy, Alex."

That was never going to happen. Not for him, anyway. "I'll do my best."

"And your best is all I can ask of you." Her eyes were a deeper blue than ever right then, violet-blue. And her lips...

Better not to think about her lips. "Well, all right," he said. "It's settled."

"Yes," she answered quietly. "We'll be married. This morning."

He offered his hand.

She ignored it, surging forward on tiptoe instead, reaching up to take his shoulders, pulling him down and brushing the sweetest, too-swift kiss across his mouth. His senses flooded with the scent of her and her lips were infinitely soft. Warm.

He could have so easily broken free of her delicate hold, could have stepped back. But he didn't.

He was captured. Disarmed. An all-too-willing prisoner.

Unbidden images flashed through his mind: Lili as a little girl, all dressed up as a fairy princess in a gossamer froth of purple and green, a foil crown on her head, a handmade wand in her hand. She wore wings, wire wings covered in transparent gauze. There was to be a play, wasn't there, one of those plays she and his sisters were always putting on? He remembered her out by one of the fountains in the palace gardens, all dressed up to play a fairy princess, arms outstretched, turning in circles, giggling with happiness, her golden head tipped back, her face turned up to the sun.

The little-girl Lili faded away.

He saw her on that fateful morning in April, her hair flowing over his hands, her eyes dazed, dreamy. He saw the perfect curve of her hip, the concave temptation of her belly. The golden curls between her long, slim thighs. Her skin that was pale as milk, only faintly stained with pink.

Now, in the final hours of darkness on the morning they would marry, he had to steel himself to keep from reaching out, drawing her close, deepening that light, quick brush of a kiss.

Blessedly, within a few seconds, she let him go. "Good night, Alex," she told him softly.

And then she turned and left him there, holding his empty glass and feeling bereft when he should have been grateful that she had gone.

Chapter Three

Lili's wedding gown wasn't white. It wasn't even a gown, really. It was a very ladylike dress by Valentino, a tea-length dress of painted silk, dotted with tiny sprays of pale flowers on a ground of purple so dark it might have been midnight blue. Her suede shoes were deep violet, with ankle straps and very high heels. She smoothed her acres of hair into a simple twist and wore crystal Pavé earrings.

At a quarter of nine, she stood before the cheval glass in her palace guest apartment, ready to say her vows.

One of her attendants entered. "His Majesty is here."

She greeted him in the sitting room. "Papa."

He hesitated, the way he always did after he'd lost his wild Alagonian temper. He looked so hopeful and abashed. "Forgive me?"

"Always."

He came to her and enfolded her in his lean arms, holding her close as he used to do so often when she was a child.

When he took her by the shoulders and stepped away a little, he gazed at her admiringly. "You are a beauty, just like your mother." There was sadness in his eyes when he spoke of his lost queen. "She looked forward so eagerly to your wedding day."

Lili kept her smile in place, though her father's image blurred a little to her misty eyes. "I feel she is watching over us, blessing us. I do, Papa."

He touched her cheek, laid his hand lightly against her upswept hair. "She always planned a large, royal wedding for you, a wedding of state, a thing of pomp and glory, at D'Alagon." D'Alagon was the Alagonian royal palace. It stood proudly on a hill above the capital city and port of Salvia. "I hope you're not too disappointed, my little love, to have your wedding in secret, to wear a day dress, to marry here in Montedoro rather than at home."

She leaned close to him and whispered in his ear, "It's never the wedding, Papa. You know that. It's the marriage that matters."

His green eyes turned dark and stormy and a muscle twitched in his square jaw. "He'd better treat you well or I'll have his head on a pike."

She straightened his collar. "Papa, stop it. Alex is…troubled. But he's a good man at heart." As she said the words, she took comfort from realizing she believed them.

Her father held her close again. "Be happy, my little love."

She thought of her groom again, of his shadowed eyes, his brusque, harsh ways. To be happy with Alex wasn't going to be easy. Still, she promised her father, "I will, Papa. Happiness is something one chooses. And I do choose it. Gratefully."

Lili married Alex at 10:00 a.m. in the St. Catherine of Siena Chapel at the palace. A trusted palace priest performed the ceremony. In attendance were only their immediate family members and several stone-faced, silent members of Alex's Covert Command Unit. Alex's men were assigned to guard the entrances and make certain that no one outside saw what was taking place within.

Later, a low-key family luncheon was held in the sovereign's private apartment. Everyone seemed subdued, Lili thought. Even her usually loquacious father was quiet. Thoughtful.

Lili was content enough with her wedding day. The main thing was that she and Alex had reached a workable agreement in the hours before dawn. She had hopes that they might forge a real union as time went by. He stayed at her side through the meal. His eyes were guarded, his words few.

But then, he'd always been the quiet one, the scholar of the family, as serious and grim as his twin Damien was lighthearted and full of fun. From early childhood, Alex had wanted to be a writer, a journalist. He and Damien got their degrees from America, at Princeton, as their older brothers Max and Rule had done before them. Damien barely got through, but Alex was at the head of his class. He published early, a number of scholarly articles on Montedoran history, on the future of his people in the modern world.

Then he'd decided he wanted to write about Afghanistan. His American friend, Devon Lucas, the one who died while they were prisoners there, had somehow been involved in that decision. The story, at least as it had been told to Lili, was muddy at best. Three weeks into his stay in Afghanistan, Alex and his friend had vanished without a trace. He was gone for so long. They all assumed that both men must have died. But somehow, Alex had survived and made it home. And when he returned, the intense, brooding scholar had been replaced by a hardened warrior.

After the luncheon, Alex went off to work. She wasn't

sure exactly what he did, but the activity occurred in the training yard not far from the palace and no doubt involved much sweating and displays of manly strength. Lili spent a couple of hours with her new sisters-in-law in Rule and Sydney's apartment. Sydney, as it turned out, was having a baby, too. She and Lili were both due in January. They agreed that the birth of a child was the perfect way to celebrate the New Year.

When Lili left the others, she went to change into a pale blue silk skirt and matching jacket. She met Alex, now dressed in a fine designer suit, in the private office of Her Sovereign Highness. For an hour, they received instructions and coaching from the palace press secretary.

And then, at five that afternoon, they were the star attraction at a press conference in the Blue Room of the State Apartments—the State Apartments being the official wing of the palace where public visits and activities took place. They sat at a long, red-clothed table flanked by her father on one side and Adrienne and Evan on the other. They faced row upon row of chairs filled with press people. There were cameras and microphones and a whole lot of questions.

Lili said what she had been told to say, as did Alex. They sat close together and held hands, as per the palace press secretary's instructions.

It went as well as it could have been expected to go, Lili thought. As usual, the press people interrupted one another and talked over each other. They were impatient, demanding—and full of suspicion that more had to be going on than an elopement between a prince of Montedoro and Alagonia's heir presumptive.

Lili concentrated on remaining calm and unruffled. On being gracious and not saying too much. She said how happy she was to be Alex's wife. And how glad she felt that she and Alexander had finally come forward about their marriage.

She was thrilled, she said, that she could now be Alex's wife for all the world to see. And she was so looking forward to the gala dinner party that night. It would be a chance to celebrate their union with the people they loved the most.

Like all unpleasant occurrences in life, the press conference eventually came to an end. The press people were ushered out through one door. Lily, Alex, her father and Alex's parents escaped through another.

Dinner, a formal affair to which Lili wore diamonds and a long strapless creation of metallic gold, was at eight in the ornate dining room within the state apartments. Lili's father and all of the adult members of Alex's family were there, plus several lords and ladies her father had invited from Alagonia and a number of top Montedoran officials and their wives. The courses were endless, the speeches and toasts more so. Lili smiled and chatted and played the part of the deeply in love, deliriously happy bride she was supposed to be.

She didn't get any help from Alex. He sat at her side in his gorgeous white dinner jacket, looking distant and severe, saying little.

After an hour and a half of that, she leaned close to him and whispered, "This isn't fair and you know it. You're making me do all the work."

He wrapped his powerful arm around her bare shoulders, causing a hot shiver to course through her, and he whispered back, "Ah, but Lili, you're so very good at this." His warm breath stirred the fine curls that had escaped her chignon. "And everyone knows about me, that I loathe any and all ceremonies of state—including endless, boring state dinners like this one. They all simply think I can't wait to get you alone and out of that gold dress."

She smiled at him in a way that she hoped looked adoring, and put her lips close to his ear again. "You promised to try."

And he replied, equally softly, "And I am trying. I am trying so very hard...."

It was no use and she knew it. She would get nowhere with him here. Later, when they were alone, she would clarify their agreement and get his word that he would do better in the future. For the moment, she gave a light trill of laughter and eased out from under the stonelike weight of his arm.

The dinner went on until after eleven. Then there was music and brandy in the grand salon.

It was well after two in the morning before her new sisters-in-law spirited her off to Alex's apartment in a nod to Montedoran wedding-night tradition. They helped her to dress in a long, white, semisheer nightgown just perfect for the virgin she wasn't. They took down her hair. Laughing and joking, they urged her up into the bed and then pulled the covers over her. One by one, they kissed her and wished her happiness and eternal love.

And then, finally, they left her.

Alex's brothers and a number of other young fellows brought him along a few minutes later. Lili heard them enter the apartment. They were laughing and singing some silly, bawdy song.

Out there in the main part of the suite, she heard a scuffle, which was part of the tradition. The groom was supposed to put up a fight when the other men helped him out of his clothes. It was all completely unnecessary, as it wasn't even supposed to be their wedding night, because the story for the world was that they had married two months before.

But the brandy had flowed freely after dinner and the men seemed to have been caught up in the spirit of the evening. The scuffle beyond the door didn't sound terribly loud or violent, though. Alex, apparently, was playing along.

And then, suddenly enough that she yanked the covers up

to her chin and let out a gasp of surprise, the door was thrown open and Alex rolled in, naked as the day he was born.

His brothers and the other men were clustered in the doorway, some of them clearly more than a little bit drunk.

Alex jumped up, looking magnificent, even with all the angry scars that crisscrossed his back, his buttocks, his arms and his powerful thighs. He gave a low, perfect bow. "Good night, gentlemen."

They all shouted, more or less in unison, "Good night!"

Alex slammed the door. And then he turned and strolled quite casually past the bed where she lay, wide-eyed, the covers up below her nose. He went into the bathroom. The latch clicked shut behind him.

Lili lay very still in the big bed. She heard noises beyond the outer bedroom door, footsteps moving away, men talking softly to each other.

In no time, there was silence.

She and Alex were alone in the suite.

Lili closed her eyes, took slow, even breaths to calm her suddenly racing heart, and waited.

After several minutes, the bathroom door opened. Alex emerged wearing the same robe he'd worn after his shower the night before.

Lili pushed the covers down and pulled herself up against the pillows. "Alex…" It came out breathless and hopeful.

He sent her an unreadable glance as he walked past the bed again. "Good night, Lili." He pulled the door open, went through and shut it behind him.

Chapter Four

Equally stunned and furious, Lili glared at that shut door.

The hot, impetuous blood she'd inherited from her father spurted dangerously fast through her veins. More than she needed to draw her next breath, she longed to throw back the covers and follow him, to call him all manner of unattractive epithets, to demand that he honor his promises to her, that he at least *talk* with her....

But Lili was not only a product of her hot-blooded sire. She had her mother's sweeter, gentler nature to call on, as well. Her mother, of English descent, born Lady Evelyn of Dun-Lyle, never raised her voice. Queen Evelyn had ways other than shouting and carrying on to get the things she wanted from life and from her passionate, stormy-natured husband.

"Never start a fight from a position of weakness, my darling," Lili's mother had advised with a Mona Lisa smile. "If you're going in swinging, make sure you're standing on firm ground or you're likely to end up on your ass."

Lili folded her arms across the front of her virginal night-gown, glared some more at the door Alex had just shut in her face, and admitted to herself that she was definitely in a position of weakness at the moment, that she was in no way on solid ground. If she went storming after him, she'd only come off the fool, the unwanted wife left alone in her marriage bed by her uninterested groom.

She had to give him credit, really. By leaving her alone in his bed, he'd made sex the issue—or rather, his unwillingness to have sex with her, even on their wedding night.

Sex was *not* the issue, she told herself firmly, although her wounded pride said otherwise. Their marriage, the agreements he'd made concerning their marriage and their innocent baby—those were the real issues. Gently, she laid her hand on her belly. "*You,* my dearest," she whispered, "you are what matters most of all."

All her life, so far, she'd followed blithely wherever her emotions led her. It was a rich and expansive way to live. But now she had the baby—and Alex, too, really—to consider. She needed to be guided more by her lost mother's example than by that of her passionate father.

Thinking back to the agreements she'd made with her groom the night before, she realized there really had been no mention of sex, or even of the two of them actually sharing a bed. So, to be fair, he had not broken the letter of their bargain—only the spirit of it.

In the morning, however, he *was* obligated to share breakfast with her. They could talk then.

With a sigh, Lili plumped the pillows and turned off the bedside lamp.

She slept long and deeply.

When she opened her eyes again, it was after ten and the June sunshine streamed in through a space between the heavy, dark window coverings. She sat bolt upright in Alex's bed and tossed back the covers.

After ten. Breakfast would be late. And her new husband had better be there if he knew what was good for him.

The door to the hallway opened just slightly.

Lili called, "I'm awake. Enter." The door opened a fraction wider and a small, dark-haired woman in gray entered. Lili yawned and smiled. "Pilar, good morning."

With a neat little bow and a quietly spoken "ma'am," Lili's favorite longtime attendant entered and drew the curtains. Pilar accompanied Lili wherever she traveled. The maid was a treasure—organized, pleasant and helpful. Also ever-available to attend to Lili's needs was her kinswoman Solange Moltano, her lady-in-waiting. Solange was a bit distant and cool. She and Lili had never really hit it off. Lili traveled without her whenever possible. It hadn't been that difficult to leave Solange behind this time because her father had spirited her off in the middle of the night.

Pilar said nothing about the absence of Lili's husband. But Lili caught the look of concern in the maid's dark eyes for a split second before she hid her true feelings behind a smile. Pilar's loyalty was absolute, so Lili didn't worry she might carry tales.

But there were a lot of servants in the Prince's Palace and news traveled fast between them. The story was supposed to be that she and Alex were madly in love. Who was going to believe the story if it got out that he avoided her bed?

Yes, she and Alex would have a lot to talk about that morning.

She told Pilar what she wanted to wear and then padded barefoot into the bathroom. Within a half hour, she was dressed and ready for the day—ready to have a long talk with Alex about the promises he *wasn't* keeping.

But then she emerged from the master bedroom to find that her groom was not in the apartment. There were several rooms. She checked them all. No sign of him. In the two other bedrooms, the beds were already made up—or had not been slept in at all.

The apartment had its own small galley-style kitchen so that the prince who lived there might have his meals prepared separately if he wished. In the kitchen, she found a large, muscular man with a bushy red beard. He was stirring something in a big yellow bowl. He introduced himself as Rufus Thermopolis. He said he loved to cook and would be happy to prepare anything Her Highness might desire.

Lili thanked him and asked for eggs and toast, which she ate at the small table right there in the kitchen. Why stand on ceremony with her husband's man? And why eat alone in the apartment dining room when she could sit here in the cozy little kitchen and smell the lemon cake Rufus had just popped into the oven?

She debated whether to ask Rufus where her husband might have wandered off to. It was probably safe to be frank with the red-haired giant. Alex wouldn't have anyone in his quarters he didn't trust absolutely—well, other than Lili herself, of course. She had no doubt her new husband didn't trust her one bit.

He also had no compunction about breaking his word to her. At the very least, he could have left her some explanation for his absence. Lili sipped her breakfast tea and admitted that she had to face reality here. Alex had crossed the line between pushing the boundaries of their agreement and breaking faith with her outright.

It was all right, she told herself, although it most definitely wasn't. He couldn't avoid her forever. Eventually, he would have to deal with her.

But Alex didn't deal with her. He ignored her. Actively. He made no pretense of keeping the agreements he'd made with her. All day, he was nowhere to be found. He didn't return to the apartment until long after dinner. She was waiting up for him in the sitting room.

He appeared dressed in black trousers and a casual knit shirt and her heart did something nerve-racking at the sight of him. Too bad his eyes were as haunted and distant as ever. She had no idea where he'd been all day and well into the evening.

She rose when he came in. "Alex." With a supreme effort of will, she kept her voice calm and even. "I'm very angry with you. This is all wrong. You haven't kept your word to me."

He actually had the stones to shrug. And he said, with nerve-flaying reasonableness, "I needed for you to marry me, for the child's sake."

Her throat clutched. She longed to clear it with a nice, long, loud shriek of outrage. But she didn't. She remembered her mother, who never raised her voice, and her unborn baby, who deserved better from her. "So you lied to me." She gave him back his damnable reason, and then some. "Straight to my face, without a qualm. You lied to me. You made promises you had no intention of keeping."

"Spare me the drama, Lili."

Her adrenaline spiked. She sucked in a calming breath and refused to give in to it. "Drama?"

"Drama, yes. Your stock in trade."

"I beg your pardon. I'm not being dramatic. I have not raised my voice. I have not picked up a single object to hurl at that obstinate head of yours. I am simply asking you, why did you lie to me?"

"I just told you why I lied. You left me no choice."

"Don't you talk to me about choices, Alexander. You had a choice. You could have been truthful. You could have told me honestly that you had no intention of ever making any effort to be a real husband to me."

"And have you do something ridiculous, like run away or stage a big scene where you swore publicly never to marry me? No. There needed to be a marriage, and with as little fuss as possible. We owed that to the child. If you're not happy with the way things are, so be it. Divorce me."

She gasped and sputtered. "Oh, you ought to be ashamed."

"I'm not ashamed. Not in the least. And as far as the divorce goes, consider the child, won't you? Wait until he's born, so his legitimacy will never be at issue."

"You know very well I don't believe in divorce. Marriage is forever."

"What can I say? So then, get used to the way things are. Go about living your life and I will go about living mine."

Lili shook her head. "I do not believe this. The way you manipulated me, that was so…clever," she said in disgust. "The way you *bargained* with me, the way you refused to read books on love and marriage or to see a counselor or a priest…"

He arched a brow. "I had to make you believe I actually intended to do what you asked of me, to *try,* as you put it. If I'd given you an easy agreement to everything you demanded, you would only have become suspicious. You'd have guessed that I didn't have any intention of doing what I agreed to do."

She did more deep breathing. "You are impossible. Incorrigible."

"Good night, Lili." He started to turn.

She reached out and grabbed his granite slab of an arm. "Wait."

He stopped, eased his arm free of her grip and told her flatly, "There's nothing more to say."

"Yes, there is. I have a…question, a question that's been bothering me for weeks now."

"Lili, please…"

She wanted to cry, to break down and sob her heart out. But somehow, she controlled herself. She held the tears at bay. "I just…I don't understand, Alex. Why in the world did you have sex with me in the first place?"

That got to him. He actually looked at a loss for a moment. But then he regained his inhuman composure. He said in a tone that spoke of limitless boredom, "I'm a man. You're a woman. It happens."

"No. Uh-uh. That's not good enough. What happened between us that morning was so hopelessly mad, so completely insane. And so very beautiful."

"Lili, don't." His voice had a ragged edge to it now.

And she refused to back off. "I mean it. It makes no sense. It's true you're not smooth or romantic by nature. You're hardly the kind who sweeps a woman off her feet. You're more the type to knock her down and drag her off to your cave. But you *are* a prince. Women love princes. And there are a lot of women—beautiful, desirable women—who find the strong and surly type irresistible. You could have slaked your lust with one of them."

He actually blinked. "Slaked my lust?"

"Well, I mean, if lust was your problem that day."

"My… What in the… My *lust?*" Now he was the one sputtering.

Truth to tell, she found his sudden agitation rather satisfying. "I'm only remarking that you could have been with someone you don't totally despise, someone on birth control, for heaven's sake."

He blinked some more. "That's a ridiculous question—or did you even ask a question?"

"I did. I asked you why you had sex with me. Why, Alex? Just tell me why."

He narrowed those strange, piercing eyes at her. They were looking considerably more lively than usual, those eyes of his. He hedged, "It's a ridiculous question."

She didn't give in. "No, it's not. Answer me."

Of course he just had to turn it around on her. "Why did *you* have sex with *me?*"

She hitched up her chin at him. "You're just trying to put me off."

"You don't have an answer, do you?" he asked smugly. "I see no reason why I should have to answer a question you can't even answer yourself."

As it happened, she did have an answer to her own question. She'd spent a lot of time pondering that one. "All right. Fine. I'll go first. I had sex with you because I was sad and desperate, because I'd lost Rule, and was having to admit that I'd never *had* Rule, that I'd believed myself in love with someone who never thought of me that way, someone with whom I'd never shared anything but a…mutual fondness. And then you let me in your door, you *listened* to me. Or so I thought. Until you finally spoke and told me how my 'petty problems' meant nothing. I was outraged then. That I had been such a fool as to cry in front of you, as to pour out my suffering to someone like you. I raised my hand to slap you and you caught my wrist and…all at once, I looked in your eyes and I wanted to be lost in them. So I was. For a little while."

He seemed calmer suddenly. And not in a good way. For a moment, she'd had his attention, raised a spark. But now, he'd shut her out, retreated behind his walls of nonresponsiveness again. "My reasons were similar to yours," he said evenly.

"Oh, please. What hopeless love had you lost?"

"Not love. Not that *kind* of love. But I have…lost."

She understood then. "Your friend. Your American friend…"

That did it. His eyes went flat. Whatever opening she'd had with him, so briefly, was completely gone. His mind and heart were shut tight against her.

He said, "I'll tell you once more. We needed to be married. That's the end of it as far as I'm concerned. We can stay married and lead our own separate lives. Or not. That will be your choice."

"I do not believe this is happening."

"Believe it," he said.

"You're a liar."

He didn't even flinch. "Call me what you will."

"I thought that… Well, as much as I've always disliked your judgmental pronouncements and superior attitude toward me, I held on to the belief that you were a man of integrity. That your word was your bond. Never would I have pegged you as someone who would lie outright, who would make a bargain and then renege on it without a second thought. But I see I was wrong. I see that I've married a man who will blithely lie if he thinks a lie is 'necessary.' I can't even trust you to keep your word. And if I can't trust you to keep your word, Alex, what is the point of even trying with you?"

He tipped his big head to the side and asked, "Is that a real question?"

"Yes, of course it is."

"Then here's your answer, Lili. There *is* no point in trying with me. Stop wasting your breath and your overwrought emotions. Good night." And with that, he turned on his heel and left her.

She didn't try to stop him that time. She knew he would only shake off her grip and keep walking.

Yes, she did long to trail after him. She hated giving up.

Even now, when he'd made it so achingly clear that he was never going to be a real husband to her, she wanted to follow him, to confront him again, to insist that he talk with her, that he come to some sort of real understanding with her. And failing understanding, she longed to call him any number of horrible names and perhaps throw some small, heavy figurine at his head.

But then she thought of her mother who would never resort to screaming fits or tantrums or displays of violence. Her beloved, lost mum never even had to raise her voice to get her man's attention. Lili thought of her baby who deserved a mother in command of her emotions. She said a prayer for patience to the Holy Virgin. And she told herself that if she had nothing else at that moment, she had her dignity.

And then she went to the bedroom Alex was apparently never going to share with her and got out her electronic reading device and read a long, delicious romance. In that romance the heroine was fearless and clever and so very resourceful, a woman who saved her hero's life when they were stranded in the jungle. The handsome, wealthy hero thought he knew everything. At first. There was lovely, snappy dialogue and things got pretty rough for the two of them. Lili almost worried that they wouldn't end up together. But by the end, love saved the day. The pair settled down to share a lifetime of wedded happiness.

Life should be more like a romance novel. Lili truly believed that.

She put her e-reader away and turned out the light and did her best not to think about Alex, about how she probably should have guessed what he was up to when he promised to try and make a real marriage with her. After all, she'd known him her whole life. He'd been the bane of her existence for as long as she could remember. He'd been telling her not to be a fool, not to be so silly, not to make up stories, not to cry and carry on since…well, since forever.

Leopards don't make a habit of changing their spots. And Alex wasn't going to change. Except in the ways he'd already changed after his near-death experiences in Afghanistan—which was to become even more difficult and distant and surly than before.

She wasn't a quitter. There was a thread of steel within her that few recognized as such. Plus, she was resourceful when she needed to be.

But with Alex, she felt stymied. Stopped. Cut off from the possibility of ever making any sort of real marriage with him.

He not only despised her, he had actually lied to get her to agree to marry him. He'd *tricked* her into marriage.

And now she was stuck. Unwilling to divorce him. Unable to get through to him.

Lili refused to believe that any situation was truly hopeless. All problems had solutions. Even this one. She simply hadn't found that solution yet. "I will find a way. I will work this out. I will get through to him, *reach* him, somehow…" she whispered to the darkness, like a prayer. Like a mantra.

But her prayer didn't seem to be helping much. She didn't believe in giving up. But with a man like Alex, what else was a woman to do?

By morning, Lili had made a decision. It wasn't a happy one. But what could she do?

She would stay away from him—for the time being. Until some new approach came to her, she decided she'd be better off to stop beating her head against the stone wall that her new husband had for a heart. She would get on with her life.

The charade that the two of them were deeply in love made it necessary for her to remain in the same apartment with him. So be it. She laid claim to the extra bedroom—the one he wasn't using to sleep in. On one side of the room, she created an office space where she could keep up her voluminous correspondence and keep track of the large number of charitable organizations to which she contributed. She sat on the boards of three of those organizations, so there was actual office work to do, as well as communications to handle. And then there were her duties as heir presumptive to her father's throne. She kept abreast of anything and everything that concerned the well-being of her country and her people.

When her charities, her correspondence and her preparation to be queen were dealt with for the day, she painted. She used the other half of the spare bedroom for her art. Lili loved to get lost in her painting. She worked in watercolors. They were so soft and transparent and full of light. She painted butterflies and secret forest glens where cute, spotted fawns gamboled. She painted the gardens at D'Alagon and the courtyards at the Prince's Palace. She painted unicorns because they were sweet and mystical and innocent. Because they were everything her cold, distant husband seemed to find silly and shallow and without merit.

Beyond the activities she pursued in her new office studio, she spent time with Alex's sisters and with Sydney, Rule's wife. At night, she had her romance novels to keep her company, to keep the spark of love and hope alive in her heart.

Three days went by—days in which Lili hardly saw her new husband. Now and then she caught sight of him coming or going from the apartment they shared. She ignored him. She had nothing whatsoever to say to him.

On the fourth day after her wedding, she was in her office studio painting a pair of flamingoes facing each other, beaks pressed together so that their heads and long necks formed a heart, when her father came to say goodbye to her. He was returning to Alagonia. He wanted to tell her he would send her lady-in-waiting to her.

Lili nipped that idea in the bud. "I really have no need of Solange now, Papa. There's no room for anyone else here in the apartment and my chambermaid, Pilar, is in and out all day, helping wherever I need her. I think it's time we…set cousin Solange free to go back to her own life."

"You're certain, my little love?"

"Yes."

Then he wanted to know if she was feeling well, and how things were going with Alex.

Lili lied to him outright. She told him that she felt wonderful and that she and Alex were getting along beautifully. She actually did feel better physically, now that she no longer had to agonize over what was going to happen when the truth about the baby came out. But she did feel guilty, very guilty, as she told the big lie about her relationship with her new husband. She also felt somewhat humbled, considering how harshly she'd judged Alex for lying to *her*.

But she told her father the lie anyway. She couldn't afford not to. Her father was too hotheaded by half. If he thought that Alex was treating her badly, there was no telling what he might do.

She kissed him goodbye and promised to return to Alagonia for a visit very soon. And after he was gone, she thought about Alex, about how he probably really had felt it was necessary to lie to her, how she knew he'd only wanted to do the right thing by her and her child.

So, all right, she could understand why he lied.

But she still felt trapped. She remained angry with him. She just wasn't willing to try again to get through to him.

Why bother? It wasn't as though he would ever meet her halfway.

That day, she had a visit from Arabella, the oldest of Alex's sisters. Belle was a nurse who had received her training in America and who worked long and tirelessly for Nurses

Without Borders, an international aid society that Lili actively supported.

"I'm going to South Sudan tomorrow," Belle said. She often traveled to dangerous places where people desperately needed aid.

Lili set down her watercolor brush and said, "Why don't I go with you?"

They were gone for eight days. Paparazzi and more serious newspeople followed them everywhere. That was the point, to use their status as royal celebrities to bring attention to the cause. More than one reporter asked Lili where her new husband the prince might be. Lili told them that her groom had "important work" to do in Montedoro and couldn't make the trip with her. When asked if she missed him, she answered coolly, "Of course."

The morning after their return, Lili had breakfast in the sovereign's private apartment with Adrienne and Evan, and with three of Alex's sisters, including Belle. Max, the heir, and his children were there. So were Sydney and Rule and their son, Trevor, and Sydney's dear friend Lani, who lived at the palace with them.

Alex failed to put in an appearance. Most likely, he'd had Rufus fix him something early and then headed off to the training yard to spend the day with his men. Or maybe not. Who knew? Lili certainly didn't. She hadn't seen him since she'd caught a glimpse of him going out the door of their apartment the day before she left for Africa with Belle.

As she was leaving the breakfast room, Adrienne caught her hand. "Lili, my darling, I would like a few words with you. My office, at eleven?" Her Sovereign Highness spoke kindly, as always. And with fondness.

Still, a shiver of unease tickled the skin between Lili's shoulder blades and her stomach felt queasy for the first time in days. She pulled her fingers free of Adrienne's and replied that of course, she would be there.

At a few minutes before eleven, Adrienne's private secretary ushered her into the sovereign's large, beautifully appointed palace office. Adrienne was there and so was Evan. Alex's mother greeted her warmly and led her over to the conversation area, which consisted of two large sofas, a coffee table and a couple of Louis XV wingback chairs. She asked her secretary to serve tea for four.

Four. Who else was expected?

Lili didn't ask. She felt that funny tightness between her shoulder blades again. And then in walked the man she'd made the dreadful error of marrying exactly two weeks before. Her stomach lurched.

And her silly heart ached at the sight of him. He looked so terribly bleak. So tragically self-contained. She *hurt* for him, for his loneliness that he wrapped himself in like a shroud.

She ached for him and then she told herself to stop it. It was his choice to cut himself off from other people—to trick her into marriage and then throw away that marriage without even giving what they might have shared a chance.

He didn't look the least pleased to see her. "Lili," he said gruffly, with a regal nod.

"Alex." She said his name as if by rote.

And then Adrienne hugged him and told him to have a seat. Evan came over and joined them. He kissed Lily and asked how she was feeling and she told him that she was doing fine.

"Feeling well?" Evan asked.

"Yes. Yes, I am. Perfectly well, thank you." She beamed her warmest smile at Alex's father and was scrupulously careful not to give her new husband as much as a glance.

Why had they been summoned? What was going on? Lili had a feeling that whatever it was, it wasn't good.

The secretary entered with a silver tea service. She set it down.

Adrienne, who had gone back over to her enormous, heavily carved antique desk, dismissed the woman. "I will pour. Thank you, Regina."

"Ma'am," said the secretary with a nod deep enough to serve as a bow. She left.

Adrienne came back and joined them. She sat on the sofa in front of the tea service. She had something—rolled-up newspapers and magazines?—in her hand. "The tea will need to steep a little," she said. And then she slid the tray to the side and smoothed the papers she held down onto the coffee table. "My darlings, this will never do."

Lili's stomach lurched again as she stared at a photograph of herself and Belle taken a few days before, in a hospital tent in South Sudan. *Princess Lili aids the needy, leaves Prince Alex behind.*

Adrienne spoke again, gently as always. "This article spends a few paragraphs on your history with one another, on how you two never have liked each other and have never gotten on. Then it proceeds to say that nothing has changed, that your marriage is a sham."

Alex cleared his throat and started to speak.

But his mother put up a hand. "That was only the beginning," Adrienne continued. "The article speculates that you, Lili, are 'preggers'—their word." Adrienne made quote marks in the air. "'Sources reveal,' it says here, that the child is not even Alex's, that Alexander has thrown himself on his proverbial sword to salvage your reputation, Lili. That he's married you to give your child a name, and for the marriage settlement you bring, and for the chance to be the consort of a queen." She tossed that tabloid aside and fanned out the ones beneath it. "These others make similar outrageous allegations. We already have our solicitors tackling this problem, of course."

Lili put a hand to her mouth. "Oh, no. Papa will be livid. There's no telling what he might do."

Adrienne and Evan shared a speaking look. Then Evan said, "We've discussed the problem with His Majesty at length this morning."

Adrienne gave her husband a fond glance. "We have a plan and Leo is willing to sit back and allow the plan to unfold."

"Papa? Sit back? Are you sure?"

Adrienne nodded. "He wants the best for you, Lili. For *both* of you."

"It's all my fault," Alex said in a low voice. He was hanging his head.

Lili stared at his big, bent head and wondered if she'd heard right. True, it really *was* his fault. Mostly...

All right, she *had* made love with him. And enthusiastically, too. But he was the one who'd tricked *her* into marriage and then coldly explained to her that they were going to be leading separate lives. How could she pretend to be madly in love when her husband refused to get near her?

Chidingly, Adrienne reminded her son, "You agreed to play the part of the infatuated and doting groom. Yet you and Lili have not been seen in each other's company since your wedding day."

"I know," Alex said grimly. "I...I have no excuse, Mother. I wasn't thinking clearly."

Not thinking clearly. Oh, please. Lili felt wonderfully vindicated and self-righteous at that moment.

And then Adrienne turned to her. "And you, Lili. Did you really think it was wise to zip off to South Sudan without your groom barely five days after the big announcer ~

you and Alex had eloped, and that you were only too thrilled that at last you could reveal your love for the world to see?"

Her face flamed. "Er. Well, I…"

Adrienne reached across the table and squeezed her hand. "Never mind." She sent her son a patient glance. "We do have a solution. I want both of you to give me your word that you will work together to make the world see how madly in love you really are with each other."

Madly in love. Lili held back a snort. Adrienne said it so easily, as though it were true.

Alex said, "Yes. Whatever I have to do, I'm willing." He sounded even more grim than usual. As though he expected to be asked to cut off an arm or go barefoot into a dark cave filled with poisonous snakes. It wasn't the least flattering.

But then, Alex had never been the kind to flatter a woman—especially not Lili.

Adrienne turned those huge, almond-shaped dark eyes on her. "And you, Lili?"

Lili sat up straight. "Yes, I understand. Whatever the plan is, I'll give it my all."

Chapter Five

"A honeymoon," Alex's mother announced. Alex and Lili were to have a honeymoon.

Alex hadn't exactly been prepared for that.

They were to spend three weeks floating around the Mediterranean on one of the family yachts, the *Princess Royale*. The two of them were to do nothing but be together. Constantly. They would be expected to indulge in endless and unabashed public displays of affection, which would of course be photographed by intrepid paparazzi circling overhead in helicopters, zipping around on other boats and trailing in their wake at every port of call. They were to sleep in the same room, the *Princess Royale*'s largest stateroom in which there was only one berth.

For three weeks, he and Lili were to be inseparable.

Alex hated the idea. It was an enormous waste of precious time, time he should have been spending with his men. The CCU needed him. And he needed them. They were h pose, the one goal left to him after the rest of his life went to dust. If he did nothing else, he could see to it that his country had a properly trained secret service ready to protect the members of the princely family and extract Montedoran citizens from any situation, no matter how dire or isolated, where they might be held against their will.

As to this problem in his marriage, yes, he knew he was in the wrong. He had gone too far. In his need to keep Lili at bay, he'd said things he shouldn't have. He'd told her outright that he had no intention of keeping his word to her. He never should have done that.

He should have been more agreeable. More…subtle. But affability and tact had never been his strong suits. At the very least, he should have kept their innocent unborn child in mind, should have protected his family from the ugly attention of the tabloids by making an effort with his new wife.

But it was hard to keep a purpose in mind when he was around Lili. Since that fateful morning in April when he'd taken her virginity, he found that she totally scrambled his circuits. She…roused him. In a sexual way. She made him weak. Somewhere deep within himself, he wanted to give in to her. She constituted a distraction from his purpose, and a surprisingly powerful one at that.

He couldn't afford distractions, so he had hurt her and insulted her. And it had worked. She had left him alone.

Which had brought them here, to his mother's office, to the disgusting ridiculousness of those scandal sheet stories and this upcoming crash course in extreme damage control.

His mother said firmly, "Our people did not see your dding. They *will* see you happy on your honeymoon. For ke of your child, for the sake of this country—and of —a long, luxurious honeymoon must take place, n where the two of you will prove to the world d for one reason and one reason only: love."

* * *

The next morning after breakfast, they departed on their honeymoon cruise. Alex and Lili boarded the *Princess Royale* side by side, holding hands. He was very much aware that they were being watched and photographed. The paparazzi were thick on the ground.

Her hand felt small and cool in his. He thought about touching more than her hand. He thought how it was his *duty* to be close to her, to reassure his people and hers that they were truly together and deeply in love.

She turned to him as they walked up the gangway, and she flashed him a bright smile, which he returned. He noted that her beautiful mouth quivered a little at the corners. She was wearing large sunglasses, the lenses very dark. He couldn't see her eyes, but he knew that those blue, blue depths would be still. Distant. Without warmth. Her long hair, thick and rich as spun gold, caught the sun.

They stood at the bow and waved. The people on the dock, a lot of them actually, waved back and applauded and called out their good wishes for a happy, memorable trip.

From Montedoro's deepwater port of Salacia, taking their sweet time about it, they would sail east to Italy and then down along the Italian coast. They would stop to explore Sicily. And then around and up to Venice. From there it was back down to Ravenna and then southeast to some of the more beautiful islands off Croatia. Eventually, they would turn west, stopping again in Sicily and from there heading northwest to Barcelona, going ashore at several small ports and picturesque islands along the way, and also spending a couple of days with Leo in Alagonia at D'Alagon. And then, at last, they could return home.

So far, Lili had hardly spoken to him. He'd been expecting her to try to talk to him, to blame and reproach him, after they finished up the painful meeting in his mother's office.

But she'd only walked unspeaking beside him, the heels of her dainty shoes clicking angrily against the inlaid tiles of the palace corridors. That was truly eerie: to spend several minutes in Lili's company and not have her utter a single word.

When they reached their quarters, she disappeared into the master bedroom. He'd hardly seen her since.

But now they were here, aboard the *Princess Royale*. They were going to be sharing a stateroom, for pity's sake. They had to come to some sort of understanding.

From the dock, the people kept on cheering.

Lili waved and smiled. She wore skinny, white cotton trousers, platform sandals and a butter-yellow shirt and she was so beautiful that it hurt him to look at her. But he didn't look away.

He had a job to do. And now was as good a time as any to begin. He touched her shoulder.

She turned her head his way, remembering, at the last second, to smile. Her flesh beneath the fine-textured yellow shirt was warm, giving, infinitely tender. A slight wind was blowing and her scent tempted him.

He took her other shoulder. She stiffened but kept her smile in place. He turned her toward him.

She came, but with resistance, as the people onshore cheered even louder. "What?" Her voice was cool, but she didn't stop smiling.

"You look beautiful today." He spoke the flattering words easily. After all, they were only the truth.

"Why thank you, Alex." The smile didn't waver, but he could see that she spoke through clenched teeth. "Aren't you the *romantic* one?"

The crowd clapped harder as he touched her hair. She didn't flinch, but the corners of that damnable too-tempting mouth quivered just a little. "Your hair is like silk."

She smiled even wider. "Silk?" she whispered. "Come now, Alex. You can do better than that."

"Satin? Velvet? Candyfloss?"

"Never mind. It doesn't matter what word you use. I know you don't mean a thing you say."

"Don't sulk, Lili. You agreed to this."

"I am not sulking," she insisted. Sulkily.

"Good, then." He curled a finger under her defiant little chin and tipped her face up to him. He could see his own distorted reflection in the lenses of her dark glasses. "Keep smiling…"

She made her smile so wide it was almost a grimace.

He leaned closer.

A muscle in her jaw twitched almost imperceptibly, but she didn't try to pull away. So he kissed her.

When his mouth touched hers, there were whistles and catcalls from the crowd onshore. He hardly heard them. He breathed in her tiny, resigned little sigh and tried not to wish that things could be different.

As always, she tasted infinitely sweet. She tasted of hope, although he had none. Of all the joy he would never know.

"I think that will do for now," she murmured against his lips. Her mouth was so soft under his.

He didn't want to let her go. Lifting his head, he slanted it the other way. "We have to give the paparazzi their chance to get a good shot…"

"Hah…" But she went on kissing him. She even slid those slim arms up over his chest and wrapped them around his neck.

Onshore, they were still clapping and shouting and whistling. People called out encouragements. He heard all that, but only faintly due to the hungry roaring of his blood as it raced through his veins.

She pulled away. He wanted to follow, to capture her

mouth again and kiss her some more. But he didn't. Something about the warning tilt of her chin held him at bay. Plus, any photographer worth his salt had to have gotten the shot by now.

"Turn around," she instructed, her smile tender and dreamy, her voice laced with steel. "Wave to your people. As soon as we're out of the harbor, we can go below and… be ourselves."

The master stateroom had onyx counters in the bathroom and sink fixtures shaped like gold swans. The bedroom had a bed almost as big as the one he used to sleep in at the Prince's Palace until he married Lili and surrendered that bed to her. There was a wet bar and a small seating area of two chairs and a table. The thick carpet underfoot was gold threaded through with bronze.

Alex took one of the chairs and watched his wife as she prowled the room, looking into drawers, disappearing into the long, deep dressing room and then into the bathroom. When she finally perched on the edge of the bed, she tossed her dark glasses on the gold-accented bronze bedspread and aimed a cool, assessing look in his direction.

He said, "Don't worry. I can sleep on the floor."

She pressed her fingers to her temples. Now she'd taken off the sunglasses, he saw the dark smudges beneath her eyes.

He sat forward. "You look tired. Are you ill?"

Her slim shoulders were drooping. "Tired, yes. A little."

Should he be concerned? "You didn't eat a lot at breakfast…."

"I'm all right, Alex."

"The baby—"

"—is fine." She regarded him steadily. "I hate this, that's all. It's just one big lie after another."

How could he argue with that? She was right. "Do you want me to go?"

She shook her head. "We're supposed to be inseparable, remember?"

He rose. "I'll move to another stateroom. I won't go on deck."

"No, you need to stay here. Counting servants and crew and your men from the CCU together, there are thirty other people aboard the *Princess*. We have to convince them all that we're deeply in love—or one of them is bound to betray us."

His men would never betray them, but she knew that. He said, "So cynical, Lili? It's not like you."

"I've had a good teacher since I married you."

He took a Montedoran orange from the basket of fruit on the table, put it to his mouth, felt the smooth skin against his lips, smelled the tart citrus scent. "Just because I leave our berth doesn't mean I'm not completely in your thrall."

"In my thrall." She laughed. It was not a happy sound. "That's a good one."

Reasonably, he pursued his point. "I could be leaving you alone because you're tired, because I'm a doting husband who cares for his wife's well-being."

"Not after the show we just put on out there. They all think we came down here to…do what honeymooners do. If you go now, it will look as though we had a falling-out. Or we were faking it."

He peeled the orange, revealing the red fruit within.

She said with a sad little smile, "I always loved Montedorans. The best blood orange in the world. Once, when I was little, I ate ten of them in one sitting."

He split the sections in the middle, offered her half. She took it and ate it, section by section. He made short work of his half. "Another?"

She blew out a weary breath. "No, not now."

He suggested, "Lie down, why don't you? Have a nap."

She folded her hands in her lap. Her lower lip quivered.

"What?" he demanded. He had that sinking feeling, that trapped, guilty feeling. "Lily. Please. Don't cry."

There were a large number of bronze and gold pillows tossed artfully at the head of the wide bed. She grabbed one and fired it at him. He deflected it neatly as she fired another. "Of course I won't cry, you big, bloody...ass. Why in heaven's name would I cry over you?" More pillows came at him.

He batted them away. "Lili, get hold of yourself."

She fired more pillows. "You lied to me, Alex. I hate that you lied."

He knocked two more pillows aside. "Lili, stop."

Miraculously, she did stop throwing pillows. But the accusations kept coming. "You lied and you tricked me."

He picked up the pillows and tossed them back toward the head of the bed. "Haven't we been through this?"

"Yes, we have, if being 'through' it means you agree that you lied and you tricked me—and as far as you're concerned, that's perfectly acceptable."

He dropped to the chair again. "How many ways can I tell you? The marriage needed to happen. You were going to dig in your heels and blather on endlessly about love and relationships and communication and *feelings* and...God knows what all."

"See?" She pointed a shaking hand. "That. That is exactly what I am talking about. You think I *blather*."

"Well, Lili, you do."

She made a series of sputtering noises and then threw up both hands. "You don't respect me. You never did. Never—and I don't have any idea why I'm even talking to you. I might as well be talking to the wall."

He realized he really needed to get ahead of her fury

at him, somehow. So he went for the painful truth. "I was wrong, all right? I was completely in the wrong."

She sat very still. And then she swallowed and spoke in a small voice. "Would you say that again, please?"

Twice wasn't enough? Apparently not. He forged ahead. "I was wrong. I should never have lied to you. *That* was wrong. I had no right to make an agreement I didn't intend to keep." *Even if I needed to do it to get you to marry me.*

"You were wrong," she said again, slowly and much too deliberately.

"Yes, I believe I said that. More than twice."

"But still, in your heart, you feel that you *had* to do it."

"I *didn't* say that," he hedged.

"No, but you were thinking it. I know you were. I know *you,* Alex. I know you all too well."

That news hit him rather hard, because she happened to be right that he *was* thinking it. And if she was right about that, was she right that she knew him?

Couldn't be. Nobody knew him. Not really.

He made his apology outright. "I'm sorry that I tricked you."

She made a humphing sound. "But you would do it again if you felt that you *had* to."

He considered strangling her, but it wouldn't be right. There was the child to think of, after all. "Look at it this way. You wanted more time with me. Now you're going to get it. We're joined at the hip for weeks to come."

"Yes, and now you've ruined everything. Now even *I* don't want to try to make a real marriage of this mess we're in together."

Strangely, he didn't believe that. Not for a second. Lili might be a royal pain, but she never gave up on the things she believed in. "Interesting. I thought you said you believed that marriage was forever."

"I'm discouraged, Alex. Very, very discouraged."

"Yes, I can see that. I'll tell you what…"

She sent him a sideways look that spoke of pure suspicion. "What?"

"Take off your shoes, settle back on the pillows. Have a nap."

"Will you please stop telling me to have a nap?"

"Things will look brighter after you've rested." He dropped to his knees on the carpet.

She let out a tiny shriek of surprise and craned back away from him. "What are you doing?"

"Here. Give me your foot."

She tucked both feet to the side, tight against the bedspread. "Why?"

"I'll help you off with your shoes."

The Delft-blue eyes narrowed. "You are being altogether too solicitous. I have to ask. Who *are* you and what have you done with Alex?"

"Perhaps I'm…" He paused. He truly did not want to say the word. But then he gathered his determination and made himself do it. "…trying."

She stared at him, hard, her soft lips a thin line. And then, with clear reluctance, she offered him her right foot. He took it gently. It was soft and small and perfect and delicate.

Like the rest of her.

He undid the clasp at her ankle and slid the shoe off, all too aware of the slim, sculpted shape of her ankle, the beautiful, high arch of that foot, of her slim, smooth little toes that were painted the same deep blue as her eyes.

She offered the other foot without being asked. He removed the sandal, sharp images suddenly popping and flashing in his brain.

Lili, naked.

Lili, laughing.

Lili, when he came back from Princeton after his sophomore year. She was sixteen years old and suddenly way too grown up. Stunningly so. He'd said something cruel to her, hadn't he?

And she had slapped his face and run away.

He eased his hand from around her ankle, set the left sandal neatly aside next to its mate. And then he tipped his head back and made himself look in her wide, waiting eyes. "Come on, then. Let's pull the covers back." He rose and held out his hand.

For a moment, she considered. Then she gave in and laid her hand in his. He cradled her delicate fingers and she rose. He thought about pulling her close and kissing her, even though there was no one there to see them, no one to impress with how much in love they supposedly were.

Because really, why not? If they were forced to be constantly together, to try and make everyone think that they were shagging their brains out every chance they got, why not just go ahead and do what everyone was supposed to think they *were* doing?

Because she's dangerous, said the warning voice inside his head. She wanted more than he could give. She wanted to…open his heart and have a long look inside. That was not a good idea. He was getting along now, getting by. There was a certain equilibrium now. The night sweats and vivid, brutal dreams no longer tortured him. He wanted to keep it that way. Some things were simply better left unexamined.

"Alex?" She was searching his face.

He still wanted to kiss her. He made a questioning sound and reminded himself again that kissing her when no one was watching was completely unnecessary and would only lead to trouble.

"That time…" She seemed suddenly breathless. "That one time, in April, you know, when we…"

If kissing her wasn't a good idea, talking about that one time in April was a really, really bad idea. He let go of her hand and stepped sideways to get around her and pull the covers down. "Rest for a while. You'll feel—"

She caught his hand. "Alex. Please. I...have a question. Something I very much need to ask you."

Don't ask, Lili. Please. Don't ask....

But he was trapped and he knew it. He'd said he was sorry for the way he'd behaved. They were getting along marginally better. If he wanted to keep it that way, he was going to have to put in some effort. "Yes, Lili. What is it?"

Her face flooded with charming color. "I...well, for me, that, what happened in April, was good. It was *very* good. Excellent, even." She looked up at him, so earnest, so hopeful. "Was it that way for you, too?"

He told the truth. "Yes."

Her eyes were indigo, deep as night. "I was...so surprised. I always thought the first time was, you know, not so good?"

He found he had to clear his throat before he could answer. "Often it can be difficult," he said, after which he felt like a complete bonehead.

She kept scanning his face, as though she might find the secrets of the universe hidden somewhere between his eyebrows and his chin. "I have another question."

Of course you do. "Yes?"

"Why were you so angry with me afterward?"

He supposed he'd known that was coming. "I wasn't angry."

"You didn't say anything, except that I should go. You wouldn't even *look* at me."

"It was best, that you left. I thought...we could put it behind us, forget that it had ever happened."

"That's called denial, Alex," she chided. "You know that, don't you? Denial doesn't work. Don't you know that?"

"You're probably right," he gave out grudgingly. "In this case, it certainly didn't."

"Are you still writing, Alex?"

He frowned down at her. "How did we get from sex and denial to my writing?"

She lifted an arm and waved it in a circular motion. "It's all connected. It's all part of the greater whole."

He wisely did not release the scoffing sound that was trying so hard to escape from his throat. "I have no interest in writing. Not anymore."

"You should. Everyone needs a form of expression, I think. I don't know where I would be without my painting."

As far as he was concerned, the world could get along perfectly well without another watercolor of a frolicking unicorn. But he decided not to share that. "There's no point in my writing anything anymore, Lili. I have nothing whatsoever to say."

"Try, why don't you? You might surprise yourself."

"I have altogether too much trying to do already, simply in dealing with you."

She reached up then and put her cool, smooth hand on the side of his cheek. Her tender touch stunned him like a blow. Heat flared in his groin and his breath caught. She... seduced him, with a touch.

It occurred to him that she had been seducing him all his life. He'd kept up a workable defense against her innocent wiles for decades. Recently, however, she'd been breaching the battlements, digging defiant little tunnels under the walls....

One kiss, he found himself thinking. One kiss unobserved by a single paparazzo. What could it hurt?

And then she went on tiptoe, the way she had done before dawn on their wedding day. She went on tiptoe and pressed her lips to his.

A butterfly-brush of a kiss, too brief. Too beautiful for words.

She sank back to her bare heels. "All right, then. I'll have a nap."

He wanted to laugh. And groan. And drag her close again.

But he only turned to the bed and pulled down the covers as she padded over to the dressing room, vanishing inside. A moment later, she emerged with an enormous pink T-shirt and went into the bath. He sank to his chair and waited until she came out dressed in the T-shirt, which had a giant-sized picture of Minnie Mouse making a telephone call on the front.

"I actually do feel a little better about everything," she announced as she climbed up into the bed, revealing an altogether too-tempting length of perfect, smooth thigh.

"Good." He rose and pulled the gold sheet up over her.

She gazed up at him from the pillows, her expression angelic. "I know you're going to leave the moment I fall asleep."

He didn't deny it. "By then, we'll have been in here together long enough to allay suspicion. They'll believe we've made passionate love."

"After which I fell asleep? How callous of me."

He sat in the chair again. "Shh. Close your eyes."

She surprised him by doing what he told her to do. He sat there and watched her. It was no hardship looking at Lili. Within minutes, her breathing evened out and she slept.

He could have risen then and quietly left the stateroom. But instead, he stayed where he was. He watched Lili sleep and thought how he really did need to be careful. It was one thing to find a way to get along with her.

And another altogether to let her get too close.

He wasn't a whole man anymore, and he knew that. He was a cobbled-together sort of creature now. He'd found a certain balance.

Letting Lili get too close could cast him into chaos. He couldn't afford that.

Still, he remained in the chair, watching her. Feeling strangely peaceful, almost daring to imagine what it could be between them.

And then catching himself, reminding himself that he was only going to learn to get along with her, to live in peace with her. They were never going to have the kind of marriage she dreamed of.

And he needed to remember that.

Chapter Six

In the long, sunny days that followed, they got along well enough, Lili thought.

They spent time every day lazing on deck, acting like newlyweds for the world to see. They stood at the rail, shoulders pressed together, and gazed out over the endless blue sea. They shopped and dined and danced together in a number of exotic and beautiful ports of call.

Alone in their stateroom, though, Alex had put his walls back up. And he kept them up. There was none of that easy sharing and conversation that had happened that first day of their honeymoon. He slept on the carpet at the foot of the bed. He was…kind to her. Even thoughtful.

But there was a definite distance between them that set her nerves on edge.

She hated it. It wasn't real. Emotionally he continued to hold himself apart from her. His public kisses were torture.

They made her yearn for what they might have together if he would only give them a chance.

Alex hated it, too, although he never confessed that hatred to Lili. Every day, every hour, every moment of their endless cruise, he discovered new things he liked about his wife. Being with her constantly, sleeping in the same cabin with her, he could no longer deny the truth about her. She was good and kind and gentle. He even began to find her endless chatter charming.

And worst of all was how much he wanted her.

It was the bane of his existence, this longing to have her again, to take off all her clothes and lie with her naked. To bury himself in her softness, to lose himself in her arms.

But he knew her. She was one of *those* women. The kind who enjoyed sex, but insisted that their pleasure be accompanied by a healthy dose of intimacy. If the two of them became lovers, she wouldn't be satisfied until she held his heart and his soul in her hands.

Unfortunately, his heart was in tatters and his soul was missing in action, so there would be no satisfying her. It was a tightrope he walked with her. He dreaded the day he stumbled. And he had a clear sense that that day was coming.

They made their slow, luxurious way down the coast of Italy. Livorno, Rome, Naples. They explored them together. They spent two days in Sicily, strolling along the Via Vittorio Emanuele in Palermo, soaking up the sun on Mortelle Beach, with what seemed to Alex to be the entire population of the town of Messina. Among the crowds they would be sure to be seen and photographed. And Alex's specially trained bodyguards kept the locals from getting too close.

After Sicily, they proceeded north along the eastern Italian coast. In Venice, they spent an evening with Damien and his current lady love, an actress named Vesuvia.

Damien was in Venice to meet with a certain race car manufacturer. His lover, Vesuvia, was over six feet tall, with acres of tawny hair and cat-slanted green eyes. She behaved like her namesake, the volcano, erupting during dinner, spewing a barrage of angry Italian, gesturing wildly with her long, slim hands. At some thoughtless remark from Damien, the woman jumped up from the table in a fury and stormed out, leaving Damien chuckling and Alex and Lili pretty much speechless.

"I'm so sorry," Damien said, hiding a yawn. "Artistic temperament, you know."

Lili gazed at him with fond indulgence. She'd always been easy and affectionate with Alex's twin. And then she said, "Go on, Dami. Go after her."

Damien gave a lazy shrug. "It will only encourage her and she already exhausts me."

Alex read the look on his twin's face—and heard the note of boredom in his voice. Vesuvia would soon be old news.

Lili warned, "Dami, you will lose her…"

Damien only shrugged again and ordered more champagne.

"You are thoroughly impossible," Lili scolded. And then she turned her indigo gaze on Alex. "Almost as bad as *you*." With that, she tossed her napkin on the table, pushed back her chair and went after Vesuvia.

Damien watched her go with real admiration. "Lili. One in a million." He leaned close and spoke sotto voce. "I still have no idea why she ever agreed to marry you."

Given that Damien had been there that morning in the breakfast room and barely escaped being impaled by Leo's trusty scimitar, he knew very well why Lili had agreed to marry him.

Not that Alex had any intention of discussing his marriage to Lili at dinner—or at all, for that matter. "I'm a very lucky man," he replied without inflection.

"You are indeed. I only hope someday you'll come to realize *how* lucky." Damien actually sounded sincere for once—and sincerity had never been his strong suit.

"Are you lecturing me, little brother?" Alex was his twin's senior by twenty-five minutes.

Damien leaned even closer. He whispered, "She looks sad."

Alex whispered back, "Stay out of it."

"So superior," muttered Dami. "So much better than the rest of us."

Alex looked into the face that was a mirror of his own and wondered as he often did why they'd never been like other twins: sharing a secret language, inseparable. Having to learn to live in the world as two distinct beings. From the day they were born, they were set on different paths. "Not better," he confessed softly. "Not the least superior. Trust me, Dami. I know that now."

For a moment, his twin met his eyes directly. "I would call that progress—if only our Lili didn't look so sad." Dami's gaze shifted to a point over Alex's shoulder and his usual expression of lighthearted indifference returned. "Your beautiful bride returns. Alone."

A moment later, in a rustle of cobalt-blue silk, Lili reclaimed the chair beside him. "She wasn't in the ladies'." She put her hand over her champagne flute as the waiter attempted to fill it. "I hope she's all right."

"Trust me," said Damien. "Vesuvia always lands on her feet, spewing fire."

"Oh, Dami," she chided. "When are you going to get serious about your life?"

Damien laughed. "As serious as my twin brother, you mean?"

Lili turned to him. Her eyes met his. He thought about drowning in those eyes. He wished that he dared.

She faced his brother again. "No, not *that* serious. Absolutely not."

Lili was getting nowhere with Alex.

Oh, he was kind enough. And thoughtful. He listened when she spoke and actually replied without irony or meanness. On deck and on land—anytime they were in public—he touched her often. He kissed her with tenderness and desire. They even laughed together now and then, when other people were around.

But the moment the door to their stateroom was shut and he was alone with her, he retreated. He remained scrupulously kind and gentle with her, but he put up a wall between them. And he guarded that wall diligently. He never let her past it, never stepped out from behind it and joined her on the other side.

After Venice, there was Trieste. They received updates from the Prince's Palace. Their honeymoon was working out exactly as planned. The paparazzi were getting lots of pictures of Lili and Alex looking so much in love. They were seen embracing on the front pages of any number of scandal sheets. The headlines were all about how perfect they were for each other, a real-life prince and princess, living the dream of happily ever after and doing it in grand style.

Looking at those tabloid photos, Lili wanted to cry. The happiness, the true *togetherness* that those pictures seemed to show only made the reality of her life with Alex all the more unbearable.

From Trieste, they turned south again. They continued on their slow exploration of the Adriatic, of the endless string of islands off Croatia.

Every day was worse, the way Lili saw it. They'd shared

that one shining moment of understanding that first day, but after that?

They only grew apart. Every night in their stateroom, Alex slept on the floor. It was simply too sad and hopeless.

Something had to give—or so she kept promising herself. But as the days flowed past, full of sunshine and gleaming blue sea and lovely scenery, she despaired. What can a woman do when a man simply will not let her in?

On the eleventh day of their honeymoon that wasn't really a honeymoon at all, Lili had had enough. If she couldn't get Alex to truly *be* with her, then she needed a little time alone. She wanted at least a few hours outside, perhaps on a deserted pebbled beach beneath the open sky, a few hours when she didn't have to pretend to be ecstatically happy with her glamorous life and her royal marriage.

The problem was how to make that happen. Round-the-clock she was surrounded by staff and bodyguards and crew—not to mention her intimacy-challenged but nonetheless ever-watchful groom. Reporters hovered above in helicopters. They lurked in speedboats ahead and astern, ready to follow anytime anyone disembarked.

But Lili was determined. She had to have a break. And as luck would have it, there were escape vehicles available right there on the giant yacht. She could choose from a small sailboat, a helicopter, or the thirty-two-foot day cruiser, the *Lady Jane*. The helicopter was out of her league and she'd never been much of a sailor. She'd ridden in the day cruiser more than once, when they visited some of the more obscure ports of call, the ones where a super-yacht like the *Princess* couldn't safely make it into harbor. The *Lady Jane* was sleek and speedy and would be just about perfect for her plans.

She should have asked to take the helm during those other rides ashore, but she hadn't planned ahead. So she decided to ask the captain for a tour and a little lesson in how to operate the controls. To allay suspicion as to her escape plans, she asked for tours of the sailboat and the helicopter as well. And she scheduled those tours between nine and eleven in the morning, when Alex would be busy working out in the *Princess's* state-of-the-art gym.

Wouldn't you know he would appear, freshly showered and suddenly way too attentive, after she'd learned more than she ever wanted to know about the helicopter and the sailboat—and before the second mate led her to the *Lady Jane?*

"That was a quick workout," she said with her sweetest smile.

Alex put his arm around her and drew her close. "I can't seem to stay away from you."

She swallowed the scoffing sound before it escaped her throat and ignored the little thrill that shivered through every time he touched her.

The *Lady Jane,* she learned, was capable of a top speed of forty-five knots. Just what she needed to get ahead of the reporters—far ahead, far enough to lose them in her wake.

Alex was right there at her side, his face unreadable, as she got a quick briefing on the controls and then proceeded down into the small cabin and the dinky head. She really did admire the nice, roomy cockpit and the helm, which resembled nothing so much as the driver's seat of one of those giant American SUVs. Lili was reasonably certain she could pilot the craft. She'd taken the wheel of more than one speedboat in her life. Her father owned several of them.

"What was that all about?" Alex asked when they returned to the main deck.

"What?" She gave him her most innocent smile.

"Why all of a sudden did you have to know everything about the helicopter, the sailboat and the cruiser?"

"Knowledge is power," she informed him loftily. "And

how did you know I had tours of the sailboat and helicopter, too?"

"I know everything you do."

"You have your men spying on me. I am deeply distressed to learn that."

"You don't look distressed."

She smoothed her hair. "This outer calm is only an act. Underneath, I'm devastated that you have no respect for my privacy."

"You're up to something. What?" His voice was dark and deep—as his heart. As his carefully hidden soul.

She heard the blades of a helicopter beating off to the east, toward the Dalmatian archipelago, the southern string of islands off Croatia. "We're being watched." She arched a brow.

"We're always being watched. I asked you what you're up to."

They stood at the rail. She moved in closer. "Kiss me. Slowly. Give them a nice show...."

He leaned down, so his fine lips hovered so close to hers. "They have a thousand pictures of us kissing by now." He smelled so manly, so clean and good. Longing rose within her, for more than he would ever give her.

She kept it light. Teasing. "Another kiss certainly can't hurt. It's our job to be convincing...."

He brushed his lips across hers—once. And then again. His breath quickened, proof that he did respond to her nearness, no matter how tight a rein he kept on himself in private. Something down inside her went instantly soft and willing.

Not that it mattered. The moment they were alone, he would withdraw. He always did.

"Again," she whispered, her lips tipped up in invitation. "Kiss me again."

He did. And that time he really kissed her, wrapping his big arms so tightly around her, gathering her into his hard, warm body. For a moment, she really was happy. She forgot everything but the sun on her back, the gentle wind in her hair—and most of all, the heat of him surrounding her, the delicious temptation of his lips on hers.

When he lifted his head, he asked, "Tonight? Is that it? While I'm asleep, you plan to sneak out of our cabin, steal that boat and head for some deserted island where you can be alone to nurse your injured pride while the rest of us go mad searching for you?"

Her heart sank. How could he know her plan so easily? It wasn't fair. "My pride is not injured." She looked him square in the eye—and baldly lied. "And don't be silly. Of course I'm not sneaking away in the middle of the night."

He clasped her shoulders. Gently, he rubbed them. It felt way too good. He lifted one big hand and touched her cheek with it, tracing the line of her hair. "You would never talk any of the crew into lowering that boat for you, no matter that you've charmed them so completely they're all half in love with you. Plus, my men will be watching. They would never allow you to leave the *Princess* without my approval."

She laughed then. It wasn't a happy sound. "Listen to yourself. Listen to what you're saying. The crew won't help me. Your men won't *allow* me to leave. I'm a prisoner on the *Princess*."

"No."

"Yes."

"This is about your safety, Lili. It's for your own good."

She gave up all pretense of innocence and told him blankly, "You say I'll drive you and the crew and your men mad. If I don't get some time to myself soon, *I* will go mad."

"Lili…"

She batted his hand away from her cheek and didn't care if one of the paparazzi got a picture of her doing it. "I mean it, Alex. I have to get off this ship. I need to be somewhere

where I can just…be myself." She pulled out all the stops and pleaded with him outright. "Please. For a day, for at least a few hours."

"You can be yourself in our stateroom."

"Yes, but you're always there with me, being…withdrawn and distant. Reminding me constantly of all the ways we're never going to have the marriage I want, the marriage I've planned for and dreamed of all my life. Don't you see? Being alone with you in our cabin is just more of what's driving me out of my mind."

"You could take one of the other cabins, get yourself some time on your own. No one will think twice about it if you want a little space at this point. For days, we've been giving them constant togetherness."

She shook her head, turned away, folded her hands across her middle and stared out toward where she knew there were islands, even though they were too far off to see them. "You're just full of helpful solutions, aren't you?" She laid on the sarcasm.

He moved in closer behind her and replied reasonably, "I *am* trying to help, yes."

She let out a tired sigh. "Did you notice how you didn't even make an effort to pretend that you aren't withdrawn and distant the moment we're alone?"

"Lili…" He took her shoulders again, his grip gentle. She didn't resist when he pulled her back against his body—yes, she *should* have resisted. But she was weak when it came to him. Weak and all too willing to gobble down the occasional crumbs of affection he tossed her way. He bent and pressed his lips to her hair. And he whispered, "If you absolutely have to go, I'll take you."

Surely she hadn't heard him right. "Tonight? In the cruiser? Just the two of us?" No, it wasn't what she'd planned. It was better. If he went with her, alone, that would be a good sign, a hopeful sign that he might actually be willing to let down his guard a little, to open up to her…wouldn't it?

And even if he didn't let her get close, well, she could walk off down the beach away from him and sit by herself and stare at the waves rolling in and away and pretend he wasn't there. Outside in the open, it wouldn't be as difficult to ignore him as it was on the *Princess*.

He said, "We'll need to take a couple of my men at least." There was something in his voice. A banked excitement.

Why, he *wanted* to go. He was feeling stir-crazy, too.

"No," she said flatly. "Absolutely not. No one else, just you and me."

"It's dangerous to go alone. Foolish."

"Oh, please. If we can get away from the press, no one's going to know where we are. We can be…invisible. At least for a little while. Oh, Alex. Think about it. What heaven that would be…."

"We are never invisible," he said grimly. "Especially not recently. Our images are plastered all over every tabloid worldwide."

"That's pure self-aggrandizement, to think that people are checking out the scandal sheets on some tiny, barely inhabited island off Croatia, panting for a chance to read about you and me and our never-ending honeymoon aboard the *Princess Royale*." Reaching up, she laid her hand over his where he clasped her shoulder. She eased her fingers beneath his and almost smiled when he rubbed the underside of her palm with his thumb. She added, more softly, "And I know you have ways, you and your men. They can track us. They can take the helicopter and follow us. They can stay back and out of the way and know exactly where we are and be ready to move in and protect us if necessary—which it will not be, I guarantee you."

"It's completely irresponsible." He pressed his lips to her

hair, a caress that felt almost unconscious. As though he'd been playing the part of devoted lover for so long it was becoming real to him. Her spirits lifted at the thought.

She said, "But you *will* do it, you will go with me and your men can keep an eye on us from a distance."

"I can't believe I'm agreeing to this...."

"Just say it. Say yes."

"Do I have a choice?"

"Say it, Alex."

He hesitated. And then he surrendered. "All right."

She allowed herself a tiny smile of triumph and squeezed his hand. "Don't sound so grim about it. This is going to be fun."

Alex knew he must be losing what was left of his mind.

He should have told her no, they absolutely could not go speeding off across the Adriatic to some semideserted Croatian island in the day cruiser. It wasn't wise. Wasn't safe.

But he hadn't told her no, because he wanted to get away from all the artifice and pretense just as much as she did.

Besides, he knew her. If he didn't go with her, she would find a way to go by herself—or at the very least cause him no end of trouble trying. For a female he'd always believed to be silly and superficial, Liliana was turning out to be much too clever and resourceful for his peace of mind.

He suggested that now their getaway wasn't a big secret anymore, they could leave the next morning.

Lili insisted it must be that night—at midnight. "Because midnight is the witching hour," she replied when he made the mistake of asking her why. "Midnight is...magic. And we need a little magic, Alex, you and me."

At that point he reminded himself that she had no understandable reason for half the things she did anyway. Her insistence on leaving at midnight was only more of the same.

He gave orders to have the *Lady Jane* well provisioned and re-inspected for seaworthiness. He made very certain it was understood that preparations should be accomplished discreetly, with the rest of the *Princess's* crew and staff kept unaware of their preparations. He also gave specific orders for each piece of safety equipment that must be stowed aboard: the flares, the smoke signal device, the distress light, the large bell with clapper, the paper maps, the extra drinking water, the fire extinguisher, the air horn and most especially the best in emergency flotation devices, including life rings, an inflatable raft and vests.

No, he did not explain to Lili the various preparations he had ordered. She would only mock him and call him paranoid and overly controlling. He already knew he was both of those things. He didn't need to hear it again from her.

He instructed Lili to dress for walking, in layers. She could wear her bathing suit beneath her clothing if she wished, but she was to wear practical, water-friendly flat-soled shoes and sturdy lightweight trousers. Her shirt should be cotton and she would need a zip-up sweatshirt or canvas jacket with hood. The night winds would be cool. "Also, a canvas or straw hat would be good against the sun. And plenty of sunscreen. And a change of underwear."

Lili laughed. "What about weapons? Should I bring my harpoon? It's good for catching whales *and* for self-protection."

He granted her a glance of endless patience. "I want you to be comfortable. We won't return until dark tomorrow. But you won't have Pilar and I don't want you trying to drag along half your wardrobe."

"As a matter of fact, I wasn't planning to bring anything more than what you've just told me to bring. So there." She actually stuck out her tongue at him.

"Lili, will you ever grow up?"

"I *am* grown up. I'm a married woman with a child on the way." She patted her still-flat stomach for emphasis.

The gesture gave him pause. "How are you feeling?"

"I am perfectly fine, thank you."

"When you speak of the child, you remind me how downright foolish this whole escapade really is. Reconsider, won't you? Give it up."

"No."

"It's mad."

She put her soft fingers against his lips. "Stop. Please. Let's not go over all of this again. We're going. It's settled."

He wanted to grab her close and kiss her senseless. He wanted…a lot of things he was never going to have.

He took her slim fingers and guided them away from his mouth. "All right," he said, resigned.

"Don't be dreary, Alex. This is going to be fabulous."

It was ten of midnight and Lili had butterflies of excitement in her stomach as they boarded the *Lady Jane*. At last, she and Alex would have a little time to themselves out in the open, like regular people. She planned to savor every moment of their secret getaway.

The cruiser was docked in the hold portside, concealed behind a hydraulic door, so no special precautions against detection by the paparazzi were required to get on the boat. Even so, both Alex and Lili wore black hooded coveralls over their beach clothes. Once out on open water, all in black, wearing their hoods, they would be harder for the ever-watchful press people to identify.

In the cockpit, Alex lifted the cushion on one of the benches to reveal the storage space beneath. Inside were orange life jackets. He handed her one and got one for himself. They put them on.

"Go below," he commanded, gesturing toward the small cabin as he took the helm.

She dropped to the forward-facing seat next to him, put up her hood and tossed her canvas hat and backpack through the opening that led to where he'd told her to go. "I'm letting you drive," she cheerfully informed him. "Be happy with that."

He sent her one of his dark looks, but at least he stopped telling her what to do. Instead, he got on the radio and gave the order to have the hull door lifted and the platform beneath the *Lady Jane* lowered to the water.

In no time, they were on their way, sliding free of the platform and onto the softly rolling night-black waves. Alex had the cruiser's engine going low and slow at first. They parted from the *Princess* like a lover slipping away in the night, sliding slowly eastward, the darkly gleaming waves lapping the hull of the cruiser so gently that the sound to Lili's ears seemed caressing. Tender. As though the sea itself welcomed them on their midnight adventure.

To draw no attention to their departure, the helicopter with two of Alex's best men in it wouldn't take off after them until later, when they were in sight of their island destination. Alex was constantly in contact with his men, so it really wasn't necessary for the men to be right on top of them.

It was a clear night, with only the faintest breeze to ruffle the surface of the sea. The moon was no more than a pale sliver in the starry sky. Once they were out of sight of the *Princess,* the night seemed very dark, the sea an endless expanse of shifting black. The sky above was silent. There were no other boats in sight.

She glanced toward Alex at the wheel. He seemed to feel her look. He turned to her. Beneath the shadows of his hood, she saw his white teeth flash.

Alex. Smiling. It was a good sign. A very good sign. She congratulated herself for planning this getaway.

As the *Lady Jane* picked up speed, Lili let the wind push back her hood and tipped her head up to the dark sky. Her long hair streamed out behind her and she felt happier than she had in months.

But then Alex said, "Listen. Do you hear it?"

She didn't. Nothing but the wind rushing by, the rising growl of the engine and the churning of the water as the boat sliced through it. She opened her mouth to say no.

And then she did hear it. "Another boat..." It was coming from behind them.

Alex eased the throttle higher. The *Lady Jane* roared and the wind blew her hair out like a banner behind her. He shouted, "Go below."

No way. She turned to stare back in the direction they had come and pretended not to hear him. That was when she saw the other boat, saw the glow of its lights. It was hard to tell the size of it, way back there, in the distance.

But it seemed to be getting larger, didn't it? Gaining on them...

"Hold on tight," Alex shouted. She grabbed the bar above the twin glove compartments in front of her as the *Lady Jane* went even faster, sending plumes of sea spray rising, dousing the cockpit, getting Lili right in the face, plastering her hair to her cheeks, down her back.

She laughed. The salty water felt good, cool and bracing.

Faster. And faster still. Alex let the powerful engine all the way out. They had to be going the full forty-five knots by then. Lili held on tight and dared to turn her head to look astern.

"It's still there, still after us!" she shouted.

Alex said nothing. His drenched hood had blown back. Water droplets gleamed like jewels in his close-cropped hair and in the light from the instrument panel his wet face was set, determined—and also somehow gleeful. He was having a very good time.

And suddenly, she was glad. Gloriously, deliriously glad. For the first time since that morning in April when he'd carried her to his bed, he was fully present, fully engaged.

Truly alive.

It was something.

It was everything.

It was…a start. At long last.

"Don't let go of that bar," he commanded. "Promise me."

"I promise." She laughed out loud.

And he turned the wheel to port, veering away from their original course. The sea spray rose up and broke over her again.

She held on, tight and sure, as she had promised him, as he led the boat that followed them on a merry chase, turning this way and then that way, the powerful engine roaring, the spray like high, white wings to either side of them. It was wonderful, thrilling. Wet and fierce and very fast. Lili loved every splendid, scary, heart-pounding, breath-stealing second of it.

She had no idea how long that wild ride lasted. But at some point she became aware that they were slowing. She glanced over at Alex.

He sent her a confident glance. "We lost them."

They slowed even more, the engine winding down to a low purr. And then Alex shut it off. The silence was endless. He flipped a switch that doused all their lights.

Right then, she realized that the slight wind was no more. There was not even a hint of a breeze. Now the air had weight. And it was so dark. Before, there had been the stars and the thin waxing moon. But now there was only gun-barrel gray overhead. Heavy clouds had gathered. Even the water lay flat, unmoving, a dark and solid-seeming surface all around them, denser and deeper than the grayness above. Lili's pulse, which had slowed right along with the *Lady Jane*, picked up speed again. She had the strangest sensation that something cataclysmic was about to happen.

Shake it off. She swiped her dripping hair back off her forehead, stood and turned in a circle. Horizon to horizon, not a glimmer of light or movement.

Alex said softly, "Nothing."

She turned to him slowly, as in a dream. His eyes were waiting for her. They were fathoms deep. She said, "It's eerie."

And then the underbelly of the clouds lit up. A fork of white fire split the dark.

Alex said, "Lightning."

Over the endless water, thunder rolled.

"What is it, Alex?" she asked.

The radio crackled. She heard the voice of one of Alex's men trying to raise them. He took the mouthpiece, spoke into it. Waited. Tried again.

But there was nothing. He couldn't raise a sound.

More lightning and thunder. The dark sky was suddenly alive with it. And now the wind was blowing, a fierce and swirling wind, seeming to come at them from all four directions.

"Alex. What…"

"Nevera," he said.

"What?"

"Thermal storms. The Adriatic gets them sometimes in the summer. They can be fierce. Dangerous to a small boat." He took the helm again. "If you won't go below, brace yourself."

She took her seat, grabbed the rail.

The wind blew harder, tearing at her. The rain increased. It came down fast and mercilessly, in giant, angry drops,

pounding her. The lightning flared—over and over, sometimes so close she feared it would strike them. A never-
ending roll of thunder boomed in her ears.

The quiet water had come alive with fierce and furious
purpose. The wind tore at them in powerful gusts that would
have knocked her off her feet had she been upright. And then
there was hail, hail of varying sizes, from pea-size to as big
as a large marble. Some of the smaller pieces hit her—on
the cheeks, on the forehead, on her hands and her shoulders.
The hail didn't last long. It turned to a deluge of rain again
and the waves kept getting higher, they rose up all around
them, crashing down on them, drenching the cockpit, toss-
ing them this way and that.

Higher and higher the waves came at them, as though
Neptune himself had chosen them, commanded them to join
him in his watery kingdom far below.

Alex called her name.

She barely heard him. There was nothing he could do, no
way to steer or speed the *Lady Jane* free of this maelstrom
of crashing waves and lightning and pounding rain, of angry
winds and ear-splitting thunder.

When the deadliest wave came for them, she didn't even
see it until it had grabbed them up and tossed them high
and curled over them, ready to swallow them whole. Lili
lost her grip on the rail. She was up and flying through the
air as the *Lady Jane* went over, capsizing in an instant, as
though it were a toy.

Lili hit the water. Her life vest buoyed her, but the waves
were so high. She would get her head above the churning
surface, and then another would come swarming over her.

She tried to call for Alex. But the sea was alive and so
very angry. She saw the overturned hull of the *Lady Jane,*
already far off and spinning away, farther still. And then she
heard Alex calling her. "Lili…. Lili, here!"

She kicked and flailed her arms, turning with difficulty in the rough water.

And he was there. He was coming for her. She raised an arm, waved it wildly. "Alex!" And then she started swimming for him.

The next wave came from behind her as she swam to meet him. It was carrying something—something hard. Something that struck her cleanly on the back of the head.

She felt the shock of the blow. The world stopped. Her mind went blank. And then she remembered: her baby. Alex.

She blinked water from her eyes and she could see him, still swimming, coming for her.

She whispered—to the baby and to Alex, "Sorry. I'm so sorry..." Or maybe she only thought those words.

A deep sadness dragged at her. Her heart ached with regret. But only for a moment.

After that, the world went black.

Chapter Seven

Lili woke to a gentle rain on her face and slow, easy rocking.

She opened her eyes. It was still dark.

And Alex was bending over her. He had a cut at his temple. There was blood in a trail down his beard-stubbled cheek. "Lili." He touched her face so gently. And his face... it was so tender. Tears filled her eyes. "Lili, do you hear me?"

She blinked the tears away, groaning, and reached back to find the angry goose egg high up, behind her right ear. "What... Where..."

"Do you know who I am?"

"Where are we?"

"Somewhere west of the Dalmatians, I think." The Dalmatians were the southern chain of islands off Croatia. "Listen, now. Listen to me...."

"Huh?"

He repeated slowly, gently, "Do you know who I am?"

She realized he wouldn't stop asking her until she gave

him an answer. "Alex." She reached up, touched his dear face. "You're bleeding...."

"It's nothing. A scratch. But you?"

"Just a bump. Something smacked me good and hard on the back of my head. It hurts, but other than that..."

"Dizzy? Double vision? Confusion?"

She almost laughed. "No more than usual."

He blinked. "A joke. You made a joke. That's a good sign. I'm sure that's a good sign."

"Oh, Alex..." The tears welled again.

"Don't cry." He said it so sweetly, so...lovingly. And then he bent close and he pressed his lips to hers in a chaste kiss that warmed her heart and told her so much. Everything. "It's not your fault," he whispered against her mouth.

"Oh. Oh, but you know that it is. We would be safe and dry back on the *Princess* right now if I hadn't—"

"No. Stop. Don't cry. And don't blame yourself. We're alive. The baby's alive...." His eyes widened suddenly and he sucked in a sharp breath. "Isn't he?"

"Yes," she promised, instinctively laying her hand over the place where their baby slept. "Yes, *she's* fine."

A smile tried to pull at the corner of his mouth. He didn't quite let it. "I'm so glad."

She had to know. "How long..."

"...were you unconscious?" At her nod, he glanced at his Submariner watch. "Not long. A few minutes."

She couldn't believe that. It seemed to her that hours must have passed since the wave and the bump on the back of her head. "But the storm..."

"It ended as fast as it came up." He glanced out over the water. "I can still see it, see the lightning on the horizon. It's moving fast to the north."

She stretched out her hand, touched the bobbing surface she was lying on. "A raft? You managed to save a life raft?"

"I wouldn't say I saved it. I found it right after I got to you. It was floating a few yards away. I managed to catch it and pull the self-inflation lever."

"That *is* a miracle."

He patted a square canvas package. The package had straps, apparently so it could be carried as a backpack. "The raft had a survival kit."

"What's in it?"

"I would guess a raft knife, flashlight, motion sickness pills, paddles, flares, a compass, maybe even some water if we're lucky. We can give it a look a little later. I also found this floating by." He held up the pack she'd taken aboard the *Lady Jane*. Water dripped from it, but it was made of sturdy canvas. It should be reasonably dry inside.

"That's good," she said. "That's really good."

"What's in it? I didn't have time to check yet. Maybe a cell phone?" He looked so hopeful. Cell service in Croatia and all through the Adriatic was excellent. Rescue was only a phone call away.

"I have my phone in my pocket." She felt for it and sighed. "Gone."

"Mine, too." He was wearing his bleak face again.

She reminded him, "We're just very lucky you got the raft and the survival pack."

"No argument there."

"And my pack has a *few* handy things in it—a utility lighter. Some water. Sunscreen. Money. Energy bars."

He shrugged. "Excellent. We can set the money on fire if we get cold and we don't have to worry about sunburn."

She laughed—and then she groaned. "Don't you dare be funny. Not now. It makes my head hurt." She started to sit up.

He pushed her back down. "Just lie still for a few more minutes. Please."

"I'm fine."

"Humor me," he said. She gave in and settled back onto his lap. "Close your eyes. Rest a little."

The last thing she wanted to do right then was nap. But she obediently shut her eyes anyway. She felt…scarily humble. And kind of shaky.

He noticed. "You're shaking. Are you cold?"

"No." She wore layers of soggy clothing: the life vest, the soggy jumpsuit and her beach clothes beneath that. But she wasn't cold in the least. "Just nerves, I think."

"Aftereffects of adrenaline, probably." He scowled. "I wish we had a blanket—tell you what."

"Um?" She shivered.

He gently took her shoulders, easing her up, opening his hard thighs and settling her between them. Now that she had his broad chest for a pillow and his warm, big arms around her, her shivering eased. Also, propped up against him, she could see out over the water, the endless, shifting dark water.…

He kissed her hair, the same way he had done back on the *Princess* that afternoon, a kiss that spoke to her of partnership, of affection, of an easy, comfortable intimacy. "Better?"

"Yes. Much." In more ways than simple physical comfort.

For a few minutes, they simply drifted in the darkness. She began to feel sleepy. She wondered if that was a bad sign somehow, if it meant that the bump on the back of her head was worse than she realized.

But then again, it was the middle of the night and she'd just been through a high-speed escape from a boat that had most likely been full of paparazzi, followed by a sudden, violent storm, followed by the capsizing of their vessel, near-drowning and a knockout blow to the head.

It was more than possible that exhaustion was her main problem.

"Sleep if you can," he whispered. "I'll keep watch."

"You should rest too."

"Shh. Close your eyes."

She took his advice and let her heavy eyelids drift shut.

He woke her a couple of hours later—to check on her condition, he said, after her concussion. They were still floating, drifting in the endless dark. He asked her a series of simple questions: her age, his age, the name of his mother.

She laughed and answered every one. Then she told him that *he* should sleep for a while. He said he wasn't tired. They drifted some more. Eventually, she faded off to sleep again.

The next time she woke, she was thirsty. Her mouth felt sandy, dry as dust. And the first rays of the sun shimmered from behind the rocky cliffs straight ahead.

The rocky cliffs…

She blinked, remembered: the chase, the storm. The raft. Just the two of them, she and Alex, adrift in the dark.

Lili sat bolt upright and let out a shriek.

Alex stirred. "Huh… Wha…" She turned to look at him. He was waking, opening his eyes. "Lili?" He blinked at her groggily.

"Wake up, Alex. Wake up…."

"Can't believe it," he grumbled. "I fell asleep…."

"Look!" She pointed at the cliffs, at the golden, steadily growing rim of the rising sun. "We're…we're *here*. We reached land," she said in a wondering voice. They had drifted into a beautiful little cove rimmed by trees and greenery. Past the trees, craggy cliffs rose all around them. The cove, the cliffs and the trees enclosed a pebbled crescent of beach—a beach that was no more than twenty meters or so away.

"But where exactly *is* here?" he asked in his usual careful way.

She poked him with her elbow. "Right now, land is land. I'm not feeling particular."

"You may have a point," he said drily.

The beach and the cliffs above it appeared deserted. She squinted into the ever-brightening sun. "I see a road, I think—there." She pointed. "Beyond the trees, below the cliffs?"

"Yes. Yes, I see it." He was gently lifting her.

"What *are* you doing?"

"If you'll get off my lap, I'll tow us to shore."

She laughed in delight at the very idea.

"Careful," he advised. "Don't capsize us."

She *was* careful, easing herself from between his thighs and then hugging the high edge of the raft, giving him room to get out of his life vest, his soggy shoes and even his coveralls. Within moments, he was taking off his shirt, revealing his beautiful, ridged belly and broad, thick chest.

She beamed at him.

He shook his head. "Here we are, with nothing but a backpack, a survival kit and a raft, stranded on some unknown Croatian island, and you're smiling as though it's the happiest day of your life."

Maybe it was. So far. "We made it through the bad part, alive and unharmed. We're safe. Someone will rescue us—or we'll stroll down that road over there and around the next bend we'll find a little village with a very nice restaurant—and lots of friendly villagers only too happy to loan us a cell phone." *And in the meantime, your eyes gleam when you look at me.* The world seemed a whole lot brighter than it had last night—and not only because the sun was coming up.

"Let's concentrate on getting to the beach first." Wearing just a pair of sturdy cargo pants, he slid over the side and into the pristine blue water. And then he grabbed one of the boarding assist handles with one hand. With his free arm, he stroked for shore.

There was no current at all. The water was still and crystal-clear. In no time, he was easing the big raft onto the beach. He offered her his hand.

She took it, stood up and stepped over the high sides onto dry land. "Safe," she said happily. "At last—and I am dying of thirst."

He grabbed her pack and handed it to her and then, after unhooking and removing the survival kit, he towed the raft all the way out of the water. "We'll hide the raft as best we can, and our overalls, too. I'm hoping we won't need them again, but you never know…." He got to work deflating the raft.

Lili dumped the contents of the damp pack onto the beach and then turned the pack inside out. It wasn't all that wet and should dry out quickly, hopefully by the time they were ready to move on. The bottle of water tempted her. She grabbed it and drank. It was heaven. She allowed herself a little more and then gave it to Alex. He sipped sparingly and handed it back. Reluctantly, she screwed the cap back on.

He said, "Better get out of that life vest and the coveralls." She took them off and then helped him squeeze the rest of the air from the raft. He rolled it up and hoisted it onto his shoulders. "Give them to me." She handed them over and stood watching, shielding her eyes from the growing brightness of the sun as he marched up the beach and into the trees.

Her stomach growled. She got one of the energy bars and broke it in two. When Alex returned, she handed him half. He dropped down onto the pebbles beside her. They stared out to sea as they munched their makeshift breakfast.

Where were they? Beyond the shelter of the cove, the sea gleamed, endless.

"Tell me we're going to be fine," she said softly, still staring out over the limitless expanse of shifting blue.

"We're going to be fine," he replied.

She turned and found him looking at her. His eyes, so often dark and flat, were brown in the morning light, brown rayed with amber. She thought of Afghanistan then. Of the years he had spent there, of how little hope he must have had after a while, of all the painful, scary things that must have happened to him there, the things he never mentioned, refused to talk about.

Four years of his life and he never spoke of it. Surely he had thought he would die there. She wanted to ask him about that awful time. But she was too afraid of losing the new closeness she had with him, the feeling of working together, the sense of companionship.

And he was already breaking the hold of her gaze, grabbing the survival kit he'd taken from the raft. "Let's see what we have in here." He undid the zip that ran around the side of it, the same as on a suitcase, and folded the top back. "Not bad…" There was everything they could hope for—and more. "*Two* knives." He held them both up for her to admire. "Raft knife *and* utility knife." The raft knife had a curved blade with a rounded, unsharpened tip. But the utility knife possessed both an edge and a point on the end of the blade. The sun caught the sharp tip, flashing. "This could come in handy," he said.

She found a brush in her pack and set to work straightening up the tangled mess that was her hair. Once or twice she brushed the bump behind her ear. It hurt a little, but it wasn't too bad. She reminded herself to be grateful that she had neither drowned nor suffered any real damage in the storm or its aftermath. As she wove a quick braid down her back and secured it with a damp elastic band she found in her pack, he produced more marvels from the survival kit.

"Water rations, food bars, first-aid kit, fishing kit—the fishing should be really good here."

"You think we'll be here long enough to fish?"

"It's just good to have the option if we need it." He went on with his inventory. "Magnifier, water storage bag, smoke signal, meteor flares *and* handheld flares."

"Cell phone?" she asked hopefully. "Or possibly a radio?"

He sent her a wry glance. "Can't have everything." The utility knife had a sheath, which he attached to his pants. He stuck the compass in his pocket and handed her the water rations and food bars. "Put these in your pack with the rest of your things." He squeezed sunscreen on his hand and passed it to her. "Put on some sunscreen. We'll set up a signal and then get on the move."

"Shouldn't we stay close to the beach in case someone comes to rescue us?"

"We have no idea where we are, or how long it's going to take them to find us. Just sitting here waiting seems... unproductive."

She had to agree with him there. They might as well find out if there were people nearby who could help them. She did as he told her, slathering on sunscreen.

For the signal, he sent her to collect large rocks and bits of driftwood, which he used to write the giant words *LILI & ALEX* on the beach, above the tide line in letters large enough to be seen from the air. After their names, he fashioned an arrow that pointed toward the road she'd seen from the raft, in the direction they intended to take.

It was thirsty work. When they were done, they shared another energy bar and drank the rest of the first bottle of water. After that, there were three bottles left. He stuck one in the holder on the outside of her pack.

"All right," he said. "Let's go."

She shouldered her pack and he took the survival kit on his back.

They went along the beach until they came to where the dirt road began. It wound into the trees, which were mostly scrubby-looking olive trees. She also spotted a few oaks and more than one cypress. And the occasional carob tree. Carob pods straight off the tree were delicious. Too bad they wouldn't be ripe until September or October. Overhead, seagulls sailed on the wind currents and the day had already grown warm. Her clammy clothing was quickly drying. She thought somewhat longingly of a bath. It would be lovely, to wash away the crusty, salty feeling, to be truly clean again.

And a real breakfast, with eggs and savory sausages and a tall glass of juice. Her mouth watered. Strange how precious the simple, taken-for-granted things like baths and breakfast became when they weren't available.

Then again, if she simply concentrated on putting one foot in front of the other, if she didn't let herself wonder where they were and when she would get a bath and a real meal, if she didn't allow her mind to wander to the big question of whether they would ever get home again, well, it wasn't bad at all.

And seriously, the islands off Croatia were a boat owner's paradise. Even if this particular island turned out to be deserted, some pleasure craft or fishing boat would show up eventually and they would be rescued.

The road climbed the hillside, not sharply, but in a gentle ascent. Once, a lizard scurried across their path. And a few minutes after that several small, wrenlike birds burst from the underbrush and took flight. About a half an hour after they left the beach, the road led them between two craggy limestone cliffs. On the other side, the road climbed sharply for about fifty meters and they found themselves on perhaps the highest point of the island. Ahead, the road proceeded downward into forest again. From where they stood, though, they could see all around them, to the blue sea on all sides. There were no boats in sight. And the sky above was a pale, cloudless bowl of blue. Not a sign or any sound of a helicopter or a plane.

Alex turned to her. "I would estimate that the whole island is no more than five or six square kilometers. We could walk the perimeter in under four hours."

The wind was blowing, smelling of lavender and rosemary and the sea. The small forest of olive and cypress and carob trees ahead seemed to beckon them onward. She held out her arms and tipped her face to the endless sky. "It's so beautiful...."

"Always looking on the bright side." He said it with what could only be called fondness. And then it got better because he moved closer. Just like that, so easily, so casually, he lifted a hand and guided a few stray strands of hair away from her mouth. His eyes were amber again. Full of golden light. He smelled of the sea and of his own clean sweat. An earthy scent. It drew her.

All those years she had thought that she hated him. But now she understood that what she had called hatred was really a form of self-protection. It had always been dangerous for her to be vulnerable to him. He hadn't been kind to her. Inevitably, he would lash out, say something cruel and hurtful, each and every time she made the mistake of letting down her guard with him.

She said, "Too bad there's no sign of human habitation...."

"You never know." He moved even closer. Her breath snagged in her throat. And then his lips brushed hers quickly. Possessively. Heat and happiness sang through her veins as he reached behind her and took the full water bottle from its holder on the side of her pack. He unscrewed the cap. "Drink."

She didn't have to be told twice. She took it, indulged in a nice, big sip. It was lukewarm but that didn't matter. To her it was delicious. So…wet. She longed to tip the bottle up all the way and drain every drop. But he needed water, too. She gave it back to him.

He drank, screwed the lid on and slid it back into the holder on her pack. Then he stepped up and turned, so he stood beside her on the road. He stared off into the distance ahead. "Look closer."

"At what?"

He pointed. "See, down there where the trees thin out?"

"I do. So…?"

"There's a stretch of brush and then another small group of trees and half-hidden in among those trees, I make out a few patches of red."

She squinted against the brightness of the sun. And she saw what he was pointing at. Her heart rate accelerated. "Roofs. Red clay roofs… Oh, Alex. There are people here after all!"

"I don't see any movement down there."

"Well, how could you? It's too far away and under cover of the trees—and come on. What are we waiting for?" She gave him a playful push down the road.

Moments later, they were surrounded by the trees again. The shade was spotty, but nonetheless welcome, and the road clear. Her heart sang with gladness. Rescue. A bath. A nice, big breakfast. As much water as she cared to drink….

She could not wait.

They walked at a fast clip through the grove of trees, easily scaling the gentle slopes of hills and then quickly descending only to rise again. Alex kept up a brisk pace and she traipsed after him eagerly until the forest thinned around them and they neared open, brush-covered land again.

Then he slowed and turned to her. "We should approach the buildings with caution, I think."

She wanted to argue that he was being silly and negative and everything would be fine. But then, she'd been so certain that nothing could go wrong with their midnight adventure on the *Lady Jane,* and look how well that had turned out. She gritted her teeth and went along. "All right. Tell me what you want me to do."

He frowned. She knew he couldn't believe she was being so agreeable. But he didn't remark on it, only said, "I know you're going to hate this, but I want you to stay here. Let me check things out and then come back for you."

She couldn't quite stifle a groan of protest. "Oh, Alex. No. Please."

"It won't be for long. I promise."

"Alex, listen to me. I don't mean to be critical…."

"Then don't," he suggested hopefully.

She tried to keep her mouth shut, but it opened anyway. "It's only, well, I think it's a bad idea to separate. I think we need to stay together."

He took her by the shoulders and captured her reluctant gaze. "I honestly don't think there's anything to worry about."

"Wonderful." She beamed him a thousand-watt smile. "We can stay together."

He clasped her shoulders more firmly. "You're not listening."

"I am. I did. And you just said there was nothing to worry about."

"I also said I thought we should be careful."

"But—"

"Shh. Listen." He put a finger to her lips. And then he actually smiled—or tried to. He made the corners of his mouth twitch upward in what she knew was an effort to reassure her.

It came out more as a grimace than a grin, but she did appreciate that he made the effort. "Give me twenty minutes."

She cast wildly about for any excuse to make him stay. "I...don't have a watch."

He took off his waterproof watch. "Here. It's going to be fine. Twenty minutes, and I'll be back."

Her throat felt tight and her eyes burned with tears she was not going to let him see. "I really, sincerely do not think we should let ourselves get separated."

"We're not *letting* ourselves. It's a choice we're making. The best choice, given the situation we're in."

"Who, exactly, is this 'we' that you keep talking about?"

"You know what I mean."

"Couldn't we just go together but cautiously? I mean, what good is it going to do for me to come after you if something terrible has happened to you? If *you* can't handle whatever's down there, what am *I* going to do about it?"

"I have no doubt you will figure out something."

She put on a smile. "Alex, you have faith in me."

"Oh, yes, I do," he said grimly.

"Then I should go with you."

All the warm amber was gone from his eyes. They were so dark. And utterly determined. "Nothing is going to happen to me."

"You keep saying that—right after you say how you need to go down there alone in case something bad happens."

He took the utility knife, sheath and all, from the waistband of his cargoes. "Here."

She glared at it. "Forget it. If you're going down there alone, you're at least taking that knife."

"Take it." He grabbed her hand, set the handle end of the sheath gently on her palm and closed her fingers over it. "I'm not going to get myself into a situation where I need it, believe me."

"So there is no reason that I shouldn't go with you."

"Lili." He said her name so...passionately. Then he drew her close and wrapped his arms tightly around her. He kissed her hair.

It felt so good. Why couldn't he have held her like this in their cabin back on the *Princess?* If he'd been holding her like this in private on the *Princess,* she never would have needed to get away. She gulped back her tears and clung to him and thought how she would never ever forgive him if anything happened to him. "I will kill you if you get yourself hurt," she muttered.

He tipped up her chin. "Lili..."

"No, I mean it. I am so serious. I'm sure there's nothing to worry about down there. And that means there is no reason for me to stay here when we should both—"

And then it happened. At long last. Damn him.

He kissed her—all right, yes. He was doing it only to silence her objections to his totally bad idea of a plan. And yet, well...

Oh, what a kiss it was.

A beautiful, deep kiss. A *real* kiss, a full-on, full-out kiss.

The kind of kiss she hadn't had from him since that morning in April, the morning that changed everything. The kind of kiss that hollowed her out and filled her heart, both at the same time. The kind of kiss that reached down inside her and found places she hadn't even known were there. Loving places.

Tender, giving places.

The best places. The ones she'd lived her whole life hoping and praying that someday, somehow the right man would find.

It wasn't supposed to be him. Oh, no. Never. Not cold, distant, judgmental Alexander. Not Alex who looked down on her. Not Alex whom she despised. It was supposed to be Rule.

Or so she had always been so sure.

Until Alex kissed her—really kissed her—that morning in April.

Somehow, when Alex kissed her, everything changed.

He held her so close and tight. His body was so big and strong and warm all around her. His tongue was in her mouth and his hard chest crushed her breasts in the most delicious way. She surged up against him, eager and hungry, and she kissed him right back with wild abandon. She wished she could go on like this forever, held tight in Alex's arms, lost in his kiss.

But of course, just when she'd succeeded in forgetting everything but the hot press of his mouth on hers, he took her by the shoulders again and set her gently away from him.

"Twenty minutes," he said gruffly.

She blinked up at him, slightly stunned for a moment. And then she shook herself and looked down at the knife in her right hand, at the watch in her left. "If you don't have a watch, how will you know when your time's up?"

"I'll know."

She tried not to roll her eyes. "But what do *I* do if you're not back here in twenty minutes?"

"Wait ten more."

"Oh, I knew you were going to say that."

He captured her chin again, kissed her once more, hard and quick. "Please don't worry."

"Hah!"

He took the watch from her and slid it onto her wrist. The band was much too big for her. If she put her hand to her side, it would drop right off. "Here." He pressed a whistle from the survival kit into her now-empty palm. "If something goes wrong for you—which it won't—use this and I'll come running."

"Lovely," she said, meaning it was anything but.

"Stay right here. I will be back."

* * *

Seventeen minutes and thirty-seven seconds later, Lili sat on a limestone boulder next to the road where Alex had left her and wondered why it always turned out that when you were waiting for time to pass, it inevitably crawled by at the speed of a dying snail inching uphill. She was ridiculously worried and very nervous and she wished that Alex would come back quickly so that she could strangle him. There was absolutely no reason that he needed to put her through this aggravation when they could have just gone on down to the buildings together.

She was so aggravated and upset by then that she didn't hear the rustling in the trees until the creature that was making the sound was almost upon her. Glancing up, she saw a flash of movement back in the trees on the other side of the road.

Her heart kicked into overdrive—and she promptly dropped the whistle. She bent, fast, and retrieved it, shoving the dusty end into her mouth, but holding off on blowing to get a better look at what she might be dealing with.

More rustling of branches.

Lili clutched the whistle between her teeth. She was going to let go with one long, ear-piercing blast if she had to.

The knife was still in her hand. Her fingers shaking only a little, she drew it from its sheath. And then she stood to face whatever was coming at her from the shadowed trees across the road.

Chapter Eight

"Maaa, maaa, maaa." The small white goat stepped daintily out into the open.

Lili almost burst out laughing. But she remembered at the last possible second that if she somehow happened to blow the whistle when she laughed, she'd probably scare the adorable creature away.

"Maaa, maaa, maaa…" The goat ambled toward her.

She sheathed the knife and stuck the whistle in her pocket. "Oh, aren't you the sweetest one?" She held out her hand.

The goat looked at her sideways, asked, "Maaa?"

"Well, no. I am not your mama, but that doesn't mean we can't be friends."

The goat tipped its head the other way. Its ears lifted, swung forward, dropped and then lifted again. "Maaa, maaa…"

"Come here. Come here, little sweetheart…."

"Maa." The animal made up its mind and came to her.

Lili knew a little about goats. After all, Alagonia had

three major exports: dates, olive oil and goat cheese. The goat—it was a doe, a young one—nuzzled Lili's flattened palm. "I'm so sorry," Lili cooed. "I don't have anything good to give you."

"Maa," said the doe, and dipped her head to butt Lili's hand.

"What are you doing out here all alone?" Lili petted the long nose and stroked the wiry hair of her flank. She had pretty little horns, short and set at a backward slant to her head.

"Probably abandoned when whoever was living in the house down the road took off," said Alex.

Lili glanced over to see him standing there, looking so big and strong and very much in one piece. "Give me a heart attack, why don't you?"

He granted her his almost-smile. "The house is locked up tight, but apparently deserted. There's an empty barn and a couple of sheds—no people anywhere that I could see. And it's nice that you found a goat. We can use the meat."

She glared at him. "We are not eating this goat. She *trusts* me."

As if on cue, the doe turned her head his way and asked, "Maaa?"

He grunted. "I see."

"And here's some good news," she said cheerfully.

"Tell me."

"Goats need water. That means there must be a fresh water source around here somewhere."

"How right you are," he said.

She dared to ask, "You found water?"

He only said, "Let's go."

The little goat followed them down the road to the plain stone house among the olive trees. There was a faucet in the front yard. The tap was a tad stiff, but Alex managed to turn it. The water emerged, sputtering and rusty at first. But after a few moments, it ran cold and clear. Lili gratefully drank her fill and then Alex did the same.

The stone house had an open front stoop, green doors at the back and front and green shutters on the windows. As Alex had warned her, it was locked up tight.

He hesitated to break in and Lili felt the same way. They both knew they would eventually have to do it if rescue didn't come in the next few hours. But still, it seemed wrong.

He took the time to remove the signal mirror, the flares and the smoke signal from the survival kit. They would keep them close at hand, ready to alert potential rescuers should they spot a boat or a helicopter. There were empty flower boxes at the two windows flanking the house's front door. He put her pack in one, the survival pack in the other, with the signal equipment on top, out of reach of the curious goat.

They spent some time exploring the other buildings. One was a woodshed. It was piled to the ceiling with neat rows of stacked wood. There were even baskets of kindling and old newspapers near the door. The other shed had bags of animal feed in it, some for chickens and some for goats. Lili found an old tin bowl and filled it for the little white doe. The goat attacked the food with gusto.

The barn had a workshop filled with tools and equipment and an ancient, rusted Cadillac convertible—with no key in sight. And no source of gasoline that they could see. Alex said that later, if they were here for more than a few days, he might break the lock on the gas tank and see if there was fuel in there. If there was, he could hot-wire the thing and maybe get it started.

She picked up a dusty screwdriver from the workbench by the door. "But first, of course, we would try the screwdriver trick."

He frowned. "The screwdriver trick?"

"Before you mess up a car, you should first try using a screwdriver in place of a key. It often works and does zero damage."

"Wherever did you learn that?"

"*Stranded with the Father of the Bride* by Lucy McFarren."

"Let me guess. A romance?"

"I believe I may have mentioned that you can learn a lot from a romance."

"You did. I had no idea that included a new, improved way to steal a car."

"In a romance," she informed him, "the hero and heroine would never steal a car if they weren't in dire circumstances. In *Stranded with the Father of the Bride,* a child was ill and they couldn't find the car keys. They had no choice but to try the screwdriver. As luck would have it, it worked—and, Alex, I have to ask. What real use is a car here? The road is badly rutted and too narrow in spots. And we can walk the whole island in a few hours anyway."

He shrugged. "You are absolutely right." His white teeth flashed with his grin.

Her heart seemed to expand inside her chest at the sight. He was so different here, on this island in the middle of nowhere. So much more relaxed than she ever remembered him being, even before the terrible years when they'd all thought him lost forever.

Here, he seemed free of the ghosts that haunted him at home. She thought of her dearest papa, of Adrienne, of Evan, of Alex's brothers and sisters, of her country and his. She knew that all the people they both loved had to be positively frantic about now. They would be sending out search parties far and wide to look for any sign of them.

Lili hated to think of them all suffering, not knowing what

had happened, with no clue of where they were or if they were injured. Or even drowned. She wanted to be found, and quickly, for all their sakes.

But at the same time, it wasn't all that bad here. They had a little food and plenty of water.

And here, they had something they'd never had before: each other. Or at least, the beginnings of what *could* be a real bond between them. She couldn't help but revel in the magic she had found: Alex really kissing her. Alex comforting her, holding her close in the raft last night, pressing his warm lips to hers, whispering, *"It's not your fault."* And now, just look at him, openly smiling at her in this dusty old barn.

He stepped closer. "You astonish me." He cradled her face in his two big, warm hands. She loved the way he touched her. Her skin seemed to come alive with every sweet caress. He threaded his fingers up into her hair, which was coming loose from the braid she'd woven to try to tame it. "I never gave you the credit you always deserved. You are not only so beautiful it makes a man ache just to look at you, but you are also brave and good, and true-hearted. You deserve... everything. So much. The world at your feet."

"Alex." She looked in those eyes of his that were fully amber now, warm and bright as the coals of a cozy fire, even in the shadows of the barn. "Alex, what wonderful change has come over you?"

He didn't answer. But he did pull her close. He kissed her—another magical kiss like the one back there at the edge of the trees, a kiss that had her heart pounding with sheer joy and her body stirring with excitement.

"Maa, maaa, maaa?" The little goat interrupted then.

Laughing together, they turned to see her chiding them from the open barn door.

Alex said, "Come on. We have a lot to do."

* * *

They got the signal equipment from the flower box and put their packs back on and explored the perimeter of the property. Out in the back, they found the generator and also a large fuel tank. Unfortunately, the gauge on the tank read Empty and the generator wouldn't be a lot of use without fuel. But the house had two chimneys, a stone one in front and a smaller pipe chimney in the back. If they did end up breaking in, they could have a fire if they needed one. And the pipe chimney had them both suspecting there could be a wood-burning stove in the kitchen. With a little luck, there might even be candles inside.

Not too much later they found the water source. There was a spring on the hill behind the neglected garden in the back. The spring formed a creek that was partly diverted into a large water barrel with a pipe that disappeared into the ground. The pipe emerged where it hooked into the house and at the outside faucets, front and back.

The road they had followed to the house circled the buildings and the garden and then wound on down to the east coast of the island, where there was another small, inviting beach. They gathered deadfall wood from under the trees and spelled out another message across the beach for anyone in the air to read. They also laid a signal fire—and then set it alight when they spotted a boat far out on the horizon. The boat looked like a big one, probably a cruise ship. Alex had brought the flares. He set off two of them as she signaled madly with the mirror.

But it was no good. The ship seemed to get smaller and smaller and then vanished from sight. Lili watched it disappear. For a moment, it felt like hope went with it.

And then Alex put his arm around her and drew her close. "There will be more boats. And my men won't rest until they've found us and brought us home safe."

She leaned gratefully into his warmth and strength. "I know. We just have to be patient, and do what we can to be prepared."

They laid another fire several meters away from the one that was still brightly burning. By then it was two in the afternoon. They wanted to take the road that wound off to the north, to circle the island, maybe set other signal fires.

But both their stomachs were growling. They each ate a food bar, and then they discussed the necessity of getting into the house. If there were provisions in there, they could really use them.

Alex doused the useless fire with seawater toted in the collapsible bucket from the survival kit and they took the road back to where the empty house waited, silent, locked up tight. Both front and back doors had dead bolts. They would have to break down one of the doors to get through. The shuttered windows provided a better option.

Alex found a crowbar in the barn and pried the hasp free on one. The casement window underneath presented little problem. They forced the latch.

He climbed in and she went in after him—into the dark, cool living room, which was furnished simply, with an old horsehair sofa, a couple of padded chairs with carved wood arms and a low, rough-hewn table in front of the sofa, which faced the dark hearth. There was one light fixture overhead and a number of fat candles in dishes and holders set about. Lili lit one of the candles with her utility lighter and carried it with her as they explored the other rooms.

One side of the house was the living room and kitchen, with the kitchen in the back. On the other side was a bathroom with a toilet and a single bedroom. In the bedroom, the ancient iron bed had a thin, dusty mattress that had been rolled back against the headboard—presumably to keep the mattress top somewhat fresh. Between the bedroom and the bathroom was a walk-through dressing room lined with shelves. There was bedding in there, stored in plastic, and other linens, too—towels and washcloths and a box of rags and stacks of other cloth items that they didn't take the time right then to examine.

In the kitchen on the table they found an envelope propped against a blue enamel pitcher. The name *Jack* was printed in large letters on the front. Next to the envelope was a ring of keys.

Alex picked up the envelope and turned it over. It wasn't sealed. He gave her a questioning glance. She shook her head. He propped it back in place against the pitcher and took up the keys.

A few minutes later, he had the doors and shutters unlocked.

"Look." Alex held up a key on the ring. "This goes to the Cadillac."

"Which we've already decided we're not going to need," she reminded him.

He tried the other keys and found one that unlocked the pantry that jutted off the kitchen on one side of the back door. The shelves in there were well-stocked with canned goods. And in one of the drawers beneath the kitchen's worn wooden counter, Lili found a can opener.

She brandished it proudly. "It's amazing that I know what this is. I took a cooking class once, but not the kind that involves opening cans. We used only fresh, all-natural ingredients. I don't believe I've ever actually used a can opener—until now."

"I'm sure you read all about can openers and how to use them in one of your romance novels," Alex suggested wryly.

"I'm sure I did," she agreed with a knowing smile.

He turned on the faucets over the deep, farm-style sink. The water sputtered out, rusty at first, but soon running clear and steady. They washed their hands and splashed water on their faces. Then they opened some cans and sat down to eat their fill. As she gorged gratefully on peaches, sardines and water biscuits from a nice, big tin, she was extra glad that Alex had managed to rescue her backpack when the *Lady Jane* capsized.

He sent her questioning look. "What are you grinning about?"

"Oh, just feeling pleased with myself because I remembered to bring money." In her day-to-day life, she had no reason to carry cash. Her every need was anticipated, her slightest whim fulfilled. If she needed money, there was always a retainer at her elbow who carried it. So as a rule, Lili never gave a thought to having money on her person. But when she planned her escape from the *Princess Royale,* she'd realized that she very well might need money of her own. She'd made sure she had plenty of Croatian kunas on hand. "When we're rescued, we can leave a nice, fat stack of bills next to the keys and the blue pitcher and that intriguing envelope addressed to someone named Jack…."

"An admirable plan." He gave her a nod of approval and ate another juicy canned peach. Then he said slyly, "I know you're curious about what's in that envelope."

"Oh, yes, I am." With care, she laid two sardines side-by-side on a cracker. "But it doesn't seem right, does it? Not only to break into this cozy little house and make ourselves at home here, but then to read the owners' mail…."

"It's not sealed. Jack—whoever he is—doesn't ever have to know you read it."

"But *I* will know." She ate the cracker.

He scanned her face, as though he couldn't get enough of just looking at her. His appreciative gaze was very gratifying, especially given that she was not at her best. She'd caught a glimpse of herself a few moments before in the streaked mirror over the sink in the bathroom and let out a squeak of dismay. She was a complete mess, yesterday's eye makeup not much more than a couple of dirty smudges, her hair all matted and flat and her nose sunburned in spite of the sunscreen she'd smeared on it. He said, "So much integrity in such a pretty little package."

His kind words warmed her heart. But she had to confess, "Not as much integrity as one might hope, to be painfully honest—and if it's a letter, it's probably in Croatian anyway, so I couldn't read it even if my curiosity got the better of me." She read English and Spanish, her mother's and father's native languages, respectively. Slowly, with effort, she could read Portuguese, French and Italian. But Croatian was out of her league.

"I might be able to stumble through it," he suggested. He'd always been brilliant at languages. Just another of his many admirable talents. "And how many Croatians do you know named Jack? I'll lay odds that whatever's in there is written in English...."

"Stop." She picked up the mug she'd filled with clear, cool water and drank it down. "It's really not fair for you to tempt me this way. Another word on the subject, and I'll be grabbing poor Jack's envelope and tearing it open in my eagerness to see what's inside."

"Lili," he teased, "who was it that told you life was going to be fair?" His voice was rough, husky. It sent a delicious shiver sliding through her. And his eyes said things that made her skin feel overly warm.

Her thoughts strayed to the bed in the other room. If no rescue came today, would he share that bed with her in the night? Would they be husband and wife in every way at last?

After all he'd put her through, it seemed almost too much to hope for, that this tenderness and appreciation he was currently lavishing on her could last. But since she'd awakened in his arms on the life raft last night, he'd been a different Alex altogether than the cruel and distant one she'd married.

She wanted to keep him—this new, kind, gentle, attentive Alex. She wanted him never ever to change back into that other Alex, the one who had been the bane of her childhood, who had cold-bloodedly tricked her into marrying him.

And why shouldn't he stay like this? It had to be much more pleasant for him, to be a good and loving man rather than a dark, tortured, mean one.

Lili was an optimist at heart. And she chose to believe that not only had her husband changed, but the change would also be a permanent one.

"Lili?"

"Um?"

"You have a strange, faraway look in your eyes."

"Do I?" She smiled at him sweetly. "I can't imagine why."

After the meal, Lili got her toothbrush and paste from her pack and brushed her teeth. Alex had to make do with a little paste and his finger.

What she really wanted next was a bath. But there was still much to do first. They spent an hour puttering about the house, making it more livable. As long as they were stranded there, they might as well be as comfortable as possible.

The cooker, as it turned out, was a fine old AGA that also served as a boiler. It burned wood to heat the oven and range top burners *and* to heat the water to the faucets. Alex got the AGA going and in no time the house was an oven. So Lili opened all the windows and both doors to cool things off, while he figured out how to work the dampers so the fire burned at a slower, steadier rate. The antique coil-topped refrigerator was emptied, turned off and propped open with a towel. It would be no use to them, not without fuel to run the generator.

The little goat took the open back door as an invitation. She came right in. "Maa, maa…"

Alex groaned. "Get that goat out of the house."

Lili coaxed the doe to come to her with soft words of encouragement. She stroked her sweet long face and petted her a little and then led her back outside and locked her in the barn until the house was cooler and they could close the doors again.

Once he had the fire properly managed, Alex showed her how to tend it. Then he said he wanted to spend the remaining hours of daylight exploring the perimeter of the island, laying messages and signal fires on the two other little beaches he'd seen from the top of the road.

He wanted her to go with him. "We really ought to stick together," he told her.

"That's not what you said this morning," she reminded him.

"This is different. I'll be gone for hours."

"So? I'd rather stay here and spiff things up a bit."

"It's quite spiffy enough for our purposes."

"Alex, it's dusty. The floor needs sweeping."

He assumed a weary air. "I can't watch out for you if I'm halfway across the island from you."

"There's nothing here to endanger me."

"We can't be certain of that."

"It's the only house on the island. And no one's been in it for weeks at least."

He gave her a long, exasperated look. "You're certain about this? Most likely, I won't return until dark."

"I will be fine."

"You have that whistle I gave you. Chances are, if you blow it good and hard, I'll hear you."

"I have it and I know how to use it."

He kissed her goodbye. It was a satisfying kiss. A deep,

lovely, tender kiss, like the one on the road that morning, like the one in the barn.

Once he was gone, she got to work. It was rather fun, actually. She tied her dirty hair back with a plain red cotton scarf from the dressing room and then she took damp rags to all the dusty surfaces. She found a broom in the pantry and used it to sweep the wide plank floors—awkwardly at first, but she got better at it as she went along. She unrolled the mattress and made the bed.

She even walked back up the road, the little goat trailing behind her, to pick a handful of lavender. Back in the house, she arranged the fragrant bouquet in the blue pitcher on the kitchen table.

As the shadows lengthened and twilight grew near, she worried a little. It seemed Alex had been gone for so long.

But then she told herself not to obsess. He was just being Alex, laying signal fires and messages written in driftwood on every open spot of land, exploring every last millimeter of the pretty little island.

In the dressing room, she found a soft white cotton gown edged in frayed lace. It smelled like sunshine. She put it on and rinsed out her own salt-crusted clothes and draped them on the kitchen chairs to dry.

After that, she wandered into the shadowed front room and stared out the window for a bit, gazing steadily at the road, waiting for Alex to appear. He didn't.

With a sigh, she turned from the window and went through the house, admiring her handiwork. It did look much cleaner and more inviting. There was a lot of satisfaction in strolling through a house one had cleaned oneself.

She ended up in the small bathroom, where the footed cast-iron bathtub beckoned her. She turned on the faucets and let the water run clear—and hot. The AGA had done its job well. She put in the plug.

It was still light out. She'd left the doors through the dressing room and into the bedroom ajar, so that even with the bathroom shutters closed, she could see well enough.

But what was a nice soak in a hot bath without candles? She found two and lighted them and set them on the sink rim nearby. The white gown, she tossed on the straight chair a few meters from the tub. And then she climbed in. With a grateful sigh, she sank into the steaming water and reached for the lavender-scented bar of soap in the soap dish.

It was nearing sunset when Alex approached the house on the same road he and Lili had first traveled that morning. By then, he'd made a complete circle of the island, laying signal fires and driftwood messages as he went, ending at the cove where they'd come ashore that morning.

He paused at the crest of the island's highest hill and he stared down at the little group of red-roofed buildings below. In the deepening shadows, with the trees so close around the cluster of structures, he wouldn't have been able to pick out the house if he hadn't known it was there—although a good deep breath of the evening air would have had him scenting woodsmoke. And a closer look would have showed him that the smoke was coming from a chimney pipe down below.

Eagerness urged him onward. He wanted to see Lili again. To watch those blue eyes light with welcome at the sight of him. But his contrary nature nagged at him, held him captive of his own regrets. He stood there unmoving at the top of the road.

He was having altogether too good a time here on this tiny speck of land in the middle of the Adriatic, getting completely carried away over his much-too-enchanting wife. What he needed to do was crystal-clear to him. He should dial it back, redefine the boundaries he'd so carefully erected between them. He should reinforce the walls he'd spent most of his life building against her, re-create the distance he'd established so cruelly and completely when he sent her away after stealing her innocence that morning in April, when he refused to answer her calls or read her letter, when he manipulated her into marrying him and then walked away from her on their wedding night.

But truly, she did astonish him.

She was…altogether too good. Too forgiving. Too generous. Too willing to try again when most women would have completely given up on him.

And she was tough as well. Resourceful. Determined. Responsible. And very clever. She was—he had to admit now, after a lifetime of trying to deny it—all the things he admired in a woman. In anyone.

And here, alone with her, in a world that included just the two of them and one annoying little white goat, well, he saw too clearly her numerous wonderful qualities. More to the point, he couldn't escape the central fact that she needed him here. She needed him and she carried his baby. And he couldn't bear to be cruel to her, not here, where he was all she had.

Eventually, they would be rescued, would find their way home, where everyone adored her and fell all over themselves vying for the chance to take care of her and the coming child. When they got home, it would be easier to back off, to return to his solitary ways, to go back to the man he really was: broken. Finished. With nothing left inside to give.

This place, this time alone with her, it was all a fantasy. Like one of those love stories she so admired. It was a world apart. It wasn't real. Here, he could almost believe himself a new man, a *good* man. It wasn't so. But as long as they were stranded here, he would pretend for her sake. He would take good care of her and the unborn child. He would do his duty.

He started down the road again, the road to Lili. He didn't even realize that he was smiling as he went.

Chapter Nine

As he approached the house, Alex's smile faded. He didn't like what he saw.

The front door was shut, but the windows to either side of it were open—and it was dark as the middle of the night in there. Not a glimmer of light. Surely she would have lit a few candles by now.

Had something happened in there? Had someone come and taken her?

Was she hurt—or unconscious?

What was the matter with him? He'd forgotten all about the bump on her head. He should have realized that it might be worse than either of them had thought. She could be lying comatose in there in the dark right now.

Fear for her hollowed out his belly, made the blood spurt hard and fast through his veins. He never should have allowed her to stay here at the house alone. And he'd been gone for hours, damn it.

It had been a stupid, stupid thing to do. Just because she insisted on seeing the world through rose-colored glasses didn't mean he had to let down his guard completely, to indulge her in her delusional certainty that most people were good-hearted and harmless, that she was completely recovered from a blow that had knocked her unconscious.

He had quickened his pace. He was almost at the front step at a full-out run when he stopped dead in his tracks.

Wait. No. Don't be an idiot. Not now, not this time.

No matter how much he needed to find her and find her fast, it wouldn't do to barge in there without getting some idea of the possible danger. He wouldn't be any good to her if he walked blindly into a trap. It would be Kabul all over again. The end of her, the same way letting down his guard in Kabul had eventually resulted in the end of Devon.

And like Devon's death, Lili's end would be all his fault.

He melted into the shadows at the side of the house. And then, while his racing heart hammered at him to hurry, to get to her and get to her now, he circled the building. Most of the windows were open—and all of the shutters, except the one to the small window in the bath.

He saw not a glimmer of light from inside.

When he reached the front again, he debated whether he should check the other buildings before going in, see if trouble waited in one of them.

But no. He'd wasted enough time sneaking around the outside of the house, finding out exactly nothing in the process. Except that it was too damn dark in there and also way too quiet.

Lili was almost never quiet. Unless she was sleeping.

His galloping heart slowed a little as it occurred to him that she might have simply decided to take a nap. That made a good deal of sense, now that he thought about it.

She had to be exhausted after all she'd been through.

And he was acting like a nutcase, skulking in the shadows, dithering around out here.

He was going in.

The back door seemed a wiser choice, somehow, if there really was an ambush situation in progress here. A little less expected than his just barging in the front. Wasn't it?

Who knew? By then, he wasn't sure of anything, except that he needed to find Lili, to reassure himself that she was breathing, all in one piece and not comatose.

He slid around the corner and tiptoed toward the back door.

"Maa, maa, maa…" Floppy ears bouncing, the white goat trotted toward him from the shadows by the barn.

He froze by the side kitchen window and pulled his knife.

"Maa, maaa, maa…"

It would have given him enormous pleasure to slit the noisy creature's throat.

"Maa, maa, maa…"

But if he did, Lili would never forgive him. So he waited until the animal got right up to him and he petted it a little and whispered, "Shh, shh."

The goat fell blessedly silent. It also pricked up its ears and tipped its head at him this way and that, as if trying to understand what he could possibly hope to accomplish, crouched in the shadows by the back door of the house.

He might as well face it. With all the racket the goat had made, any possible element of surprise had now been thoroughly lost to him. He might as well just march up to the front door, shove it open and yell, *Lili? Where in bloody hell are you?*

He was just about to do exactly that when the golden glow of a candle appeared in the kitchen window. He dropped to his ass on the ground.

"Maa?" asked the goat.

Lili stuck her head out the window and frowned down at him. "Alex? What are you doing out there with that goat?"

He closed his eyes and counted to ten.

"Alex?"

"Maaa?"

He pushed himself upright. "It's a long story." The candle lit up her face, made her look like an angel, sweet and otherworldly, pure beyond bearing. The scent of her drifted to him, clean. Fresh. Hinting of lavender. He spoke around the sudden lump in his throat. "You've had a bath."

"I have. Envious?"

"Green with it."

"Well, come in, then. You can have one yourself."

She was standing in the open doorway when he went up the steps to go in, holding the fat candle, dressed in a white nightgown she must have found in the dressing room, with a fringed blue shawl around her shoulders. "You were gone forever. It has to be well after nine."

"It's almost ten." Back the way he had come, the last gleam of orange had vanished from the horizon. Days were long in the Adriatic summer. "I'm sorry. I shouldn't have taken so long."

"Well," she said with a shrug, "you're here and safe. That's what matters." She stepped aside so he could enter. "I'll go and fill the tub. Would you light more candles?"

He made a sound of agreement—and caught her shoulder before she could turn for the bathroom. "Lili..."

She stopped, tipped up her impossibly beautiful face to him. Smiled. "Hmm?"

His arms ached to hold her, but he was covered in salt grime and he smelled of a day's worth of clambering over limestone outcroppings, hauling wood and setting signal fires. He'd only get her dirty all over again.

Plus, he'd already given in to kissing her more than once that day. If he didn't watch himself, he'd be indulging in a lot more than kissing—or at least, he'd be putting moves on her in *hopes* of indulging in a lot more than kissing.

He wouldn't blame her in the least if she turned him down flat. He deserved to be turned down flat.

But she was a generous, big-hearted woman and whenever he kissed her, she forgave him all over again for all his transgressions against her. She forgave him....

And she kissed him back in such a way that he had a very strong feeling she would not be averse to indulging in a whole lot more than kissing. And as each hour passed since they had left the *Princess Royale,* he was finding it harder and harder to remember exactly why they *shouldn't* indulge in a whole lot more than kissing.

After all, she *was* his wife. And while they were stranded here, he'd set himself the not-the-least-difficult task of making the experience as painless as possible for her, of being kind and gentle to her. Of treating her with tenderness, the way he couldn't afford to do in the "real" world.

And they certainly didn't have to worry about an unexpected pregnancy. The goat was out of the barn on that issue.

"Alex?" She reached up, caressed his beard-scratchy face in the sweetest, most affectionate way. "What is it?"

He coughed to clear the tightness from his throat and steeled himself not to grab that little hand and shower kisses upon it. "Nothing. More candles? I'll get them...."

He took off his clothes and left them where they fell. They couldn't get much dirtier than they already were.

The tub was small, but the water was wonderfully hot. Lili had left him a towel on the chair and four candles, two on the sink and two on the little cabinet by the door to the walk-through dressing room. There was lavender-scented homemade soap and a loofah. He got to work scrubbing off the grime.

When he was done, he shut his eyes, allowed his head to fall back. The water grew cool around him and images of Lili filled his mind. He must have dropped off to sleep because he woke to the touch of her hand on his shoulder.

"Lili…" He opened his eyes and the room was soft with golden candlelight. He had been dreaming of her. At least, with his knees up practically around his ears, she couldn't see what was going on under the water, couldn't see how much he ached for her.

For her soft, smooth little body, her luscious, willing mouth. For everything he wished they could have.

For everything they would never have.

She was behind him, a small, soft hand on either shoulder now. "Just came to check on you." She rubbed, working the knotted muscles. Her hands were stronger than they looked. He couldn't hold back a low moan of pleasure as she massaged the tension and tiredness away. "I wanted to be sure you hadn't drowned…." Her breath teased his ear.

"I fell asleep," he gruffly confessed.

"Not surprising. It's been a long, long day."

Water sloshed as he sat up and bent his head. "To the left a little…there. Yes. Right…there…."

"Did you explore the whole island?"

"Pretty close."

"Got a signal fire set on every smallest hint of beach?"

"Yes, I did. And I saw another boat. But it got away like that cruise ship. I signaled it with the mirror and used another flare and cursed the fact that I'd yet to lay a signal fire on the beach where I was standing. I watched as it got smaller and smaller until it vanished over the horizon."

"It's all right," she said.

"No, it's not."

"Alex, they'll find us."

"I know." He rolled his lowered head from side to side as she kept on rubbing at the muscles of his upper back, easing the tension away to nothing. Now, with her hands on him, in the soft candlelight, just the two of them, he could almost wish they might never be found. That it could be just him and Lili indefinitely. He could almost wish that no one would ever come for them, that the candles and the canned goods could last forever.

Just the two of them—and their baby, too, later—stranded together in the cozy stone house, where he was someone different, someone better. Someone happy. Where the unforgivable sins of the past could never find him.

Her lips brushed the side of his neck, leaving the sweetest heat, a burning so good he couldn't breathe for a moment. She whispered, "Sometimes I wish…"

He moved his shoulders under her rubbing hands, enjoying the pressure, the pain that loosened, eased, morphed into pleasure. "You wish what?"

"That we would never ever be found. That we could just stay here, you and me, in this sweet little house, on this perfect little island."

It was so exactly what he'd been thinking, he almost agreed with her automatically. But he caught himself in time. "No, you have a whole country to rule one day. And a father who loves you…" And his sisters and brothers, his mother and father. They all adored her. Everyone adored Lili. She was that kind of person. Lovable. Good.

"I know," she said so softly with a tender edge of regret. "And your family, how they would suffer to lose you all over again. And then there's the baby."

"Mustn't forget the baby," he agreed.

"She deserves the best of everything."

"Yes, he absolutely does…."

She chuckled low, a husky sound that made him harder than ever beneath the cooling water of the bath. "Oh, Alex." And then she slid one hand around to caress the side of his face with a light but insistent pressure.

He turned where she guided him. Her sweet lips were waiting.

"Scratchy," she whispered against his mouth, her hand still stroking his stubbly cheek. "But nice…"

"Sorry." He turned a little more so he could brush his lips back and forth across hers. "No razor…"

"It's all right. It's scratchy in a very exciting way."

He settled his mouth more firmly on hers. She sighed and opened for him. He tasted her sweetness, the wet silk within, and she rose, bending over him, taking control of the kiss, nipping at his tongue a little, sucking it deeper inside.

She moaned and he made a low sound in response, lifting his hand to her hair, running his fingers down along the satiny strands, gathering the golden mass in his fist, loving the rich, silky feel of it, and keeping it from falling in the bathwater at the same time.

When she lifted away, he wanted to hold her there, wanted to kiss her some more, to pull her down into the tub with him. Yes, it was too small for both of them, but they could make it work.

Maybe. If she sat on his lap….

He groaned at just the thought of that.

But then she was rising to stand above him, her eyes jewel-blue, deep as oceans, a soft smile curving that beautiful mouth. He unwound his hand from her hair and let her go with great reluctance.

She gazed down at him, those eyes midnight-blue. "We need to eat something."

He knew she was right. "I suppose…"

She took the towel from the chair and held it open for him. "Come on."

He hesitated to stand up. The kiss they'd shared had served only to intensify the arousal that dreaming of her had started. And that other Alex—the *real* Alex—wouldn't want her to see her power over him.

But then, what did it matter? The barriers he'd worked so hard to keep between them were gone now. Shattered. Blasted away as though they had never been. He would worry about rebuilding the walls later, when they were rescued, on their return to Montedoro. The water sloshed over the sides of the tub as he rose.

Her gaze moved over him, tender as any caress. "Come on," she said again.

He did as she bade him, stepping from the tub and into the embrace of the open towel. She wrapped it around him, rubbed his shoulders a little, before relinquishing it to him and stepping back.

As he dried himself, he noticed his scattered clothes were gone. "What did you do with my pants?"

"I washed them. And your shirt and your underwear. They were dirty. They'll be dry by morning."

He frowned. "I must have dozed off for longer than I thought."

"Oh, yes. I tiptoed in. I was very quiet as I gathered up your things. But you were dead to the world. I would say you had at least a half hour's nap—and what are you grinning at?"

"You. Princess Lili, the laundress."

She picked up the skirt of her borrowed nightgown and curtsied. "I shall be a real housewife before you know it."

"I believe you might. And I don't suppose you found any extra pants while you puttered about, dusting and sweeping?"

"I did, yes." She held up a finger. "Wait right there." She

vanished into the dressing room and came back with a pair of worn, baggy jeans. He took them from her and put them on. They were too short and a bit loose around the waist, but they were better than going naked or wrapping himself in the towel. "There are some old shirts, too," she offered. "One printed with giant orange hibiscus flowers, another with horizontal black-and-white stripes."

The night was mild and the AGA still burned in the kitchen, keeping the house quite warm. "This will do, thanks."

She grabbed his hand. "Come to the kitchen, then. I'm starving."

They had canned pears, little canned sausages, a can of baked beans she'd heated on the AGA and all the water they could drink.

He said, "Tomorrow, I'll try my luck with the fishing kit from the survival pack."

She swallowed a bite of sausage and a look of concern drew her dark gold brows together. "Fish. That means there will be cooking, doesn't it? Real cooking, more than just warming up a can."

He arranged his face in a solemn expression to mirror hers. "There will be cooking, yes."

"Hmm." Looking very serious, she considered. "Remember that cooking class I mentioned?" She waited for him to make a vague sound in the affirmative and then explained, "It was a French cooking class. We did lobster thermidor, chicken cordon bleu, coq au vin and beef bourguignon. But never just plain fish." She was frowning intently now, deep in thought. "I would imagine one might use a frying pan, wouldn't you think? There's one on that shelf above the AGA. Yes. A frying pan. And butter to keep it from sticking— it's too bad that we have no butter." She brightened a little. "Olive oil might do. There's a can of olive oil in the pantry."

He'd never been able to resist teasing her. "Before the cooking, you have to clean them—slit them open down the belly and remove the guts."

She had been about to go to work on another sausage, but she set it back on her plate instead and chided in her most regal tone, "I don't believe I wish to discuss the removal of guts over dinner."

"I suppose not." He forked up half a pear, bit off one side, chewed and swallowed. "It's a dirty, slimy, smelly job cleaning fish."

"I'm so sorry to hear that—for your sake. Because I'm going to let *you* do the cleaning. And I know you are trying to torment me, Alex. It's childish, you know that."

"I know, but I enjoy tormenting you." Once, when she was five and he was nine, he had chased her through the statuary garden at the Prince's Palace brandishing a headless snake. "And another thing about cleaning fish, you have to really dig around in there, make sure you get every last sticky bit of intestine out."

She wrinkled up her fine, patrician nose at him. "You are impossible."

"So I've been told."

"Next you'll be calling me Silly Lili."

"I just might." He ate the other end of the pear half.

She straightened her shoulders. "Fine. Go ahead. Torture me with stories of disemboweled fish, call me Silly Lili. I'm not going to give you the satisfaction of bursting into tears— or running away screaming. In case you haven't noticed, Alex, I'm not a little girl anymore."

He gazed at her. At length. It was pure pleasure gazing at Lili. It always had been, although he'd spent most of his life denying that fact. In the candlelight, her skin seemed to glow from within, her eyes shone cobalt-blue and her gold-tipped eyelashes were impossibly long and thick. "No, Lili," he said softly, "you're not a little girl. Not anymore...."

"Well, then. Stop treating me like one." She reached for her water glass. "And stop behaving like a bratty little boy."

He caught her hand, brought her fingers to his lips and kissed the tips one by one. Just touching her hand excited him. And heat seemed to shimmer in the air between them.

She whispered, "Alex..."

And then they were both rising, reaching. She laughed as she fell against him. He gathered her close, dipped his head and took her mouth. She tasted of pears and tender desire. She smelled of sunshine and fresh air and crushed lavender. And she felt like heaven in his arms.

He couldn't resist her. He *refused* to resist her.

Not now. Not here. Not tonight.

Yes, it was foolish. He knew it. He should maintain at least this one barrier between them. He didn't need her in his arms to keep her safe.

He didn't need...

But that wasn't true. He *did* need. He needed *her*. He needed the cool velvet of her flesh under his hand, the scent of her filling him, the sound of her sighs and her laughter seducing him. The touch of her hands against his chest, the warm silk of her hair, falling, sliding against his shoulder, a golden veil along his arm.

"Lili..." He framed her face between his hands. "Lili..."

And she whispered, "Yes. Oh, Alex, yes..."

Yes. It was the only word. The word that mattered. The word that bound them. Made them one.

At least for now.

For tonight.

For whatever nights they might have until the real world came to claim them.

He bent enough to slide an arm beneath her knees.

She laughed as he scooped her up and lifted her high into his arms.

"Oh, Alex," she whispered. "At last." She buried her face against his neck, pressed her soft lips to the side of his throat. And then she looked up at him again. "Wait."

He kissed the tip of her nose. "What?"

"The candle..." It was a fat one, with a big wick. She'd used an old dish for a base. He turned her, so she could pick up the dish. She held it out in front of them. "All right. Let's go."

He didn't have to be told twice. He headed for the bedroom, with her in his arms. She held the candle out in front of them, so the golden light could lead the way.

Chapter Ten

In the bedroom, he took her to the edge of the bed and turned again, bending at the knees so she could set the candle on the roughly made bedside table. Then he gently laid her down.

She gazed up at him so trustingly, her hair a golden halo, her eyes a strange and marvelous shade of deepest violet in the soft candlelight. "Alex, it's been too long."

He had that one word. The word that mattered. "Yes." Swiftly, he shucked off his too-short borrowed jeans.

He wanted to join her, to take her in his arms again.

But he also couldn't seem to get enough of just looking at her, just knowing that for now at least, she belonged to him, truly. Openly.

And he belonged to her.

He belonged...

It was the most important thing. For once in his life. To simply belong.

It seemed to him that never ever until now, had he belonged. All his life he had been the outsider, bound truly to no one. Not even his twin.

Until now. Until Lili.

She sat up. He knew a moment of stark fear. Of aching loneliness. He was sure she would slide off the bed and walk away from him.

But then she grabbed the hem of the worn white gown, lifted her hips enough to free it from under her—and pulled it off over her head. It disappeared over the far side of the bed. Her shining hair fell about her shoulders, down her back and over her round, perfect, pink-tipped breasts. She was just so unbelievably beautiful, almost otherworldly in her golden perfection.

Laughing, she beckoned him, crooking a finger.

He needed no more encouragement. He went down to the bed with her, the old springs beneath the mattress creaking as they took his weight.

She curved her hand around the nape of his neck, pulled him close and kissed him, a soft brush of her lips to his. "It's a noisy old bed, I'm afraid."

He kissed her cheek, her nose, the other cheek. "I'm not complaining."

"What's gotten into you? You're becoming so good-natured, so easy to please. You're not at all the angry, unsatisfied, aloof Alex I've always known."

He kissed her lips, fast and hard. "It's all your fault. You've cast a spell on me. You've made me into what can only be called a nice person." *For now, anyway.*

"I have? How very clever of me."

He took her velvety shoulders, guided her down to the pillow again. "I want to kiss you all over."

She assumed her most queenly expression. "I will allow that."

He cradled one of those round, sweet breasts. "I was hoping you might...." And then he lowered his head and captured the nipple.

She gasped, so sweetly, and he felt her cool, soft fingers threading into his hair. "Alex..."

He indulged himself in the taste of her, sucking, drawing the little bud of flesh against his teeth, then rolling his tongue around it and sucking some more until she clutched him closer and arched her back, lifting up off the mattress, trying to get closer still.

She made a low, pleading sound deep in her throat as he moved to the other breast. He took care to lavish the same attention on it. And then, remembering his promise to kiss her everywhere, he licked his way up to her throat, scraped it with his teeth, drew on the smooth, lavender-scented flesh— not hard, just enough to make her moan and whisper his name again.

He moved on, higher still, to the pure, clean line of her jaw, the sweet jut of her chin, the tempting lobe of her delicate little ear. With small, nipping kisses, he attended to her temples, her forehead, the sleek dark gold brows, that adorable, queenly nose. And then there were her cheeks, her other ear, the smooth line of her neck, that tender indentation between her collarbones...

It took him a while to kiss her all over. And he didn't hurry the task. With his lips and his tongue and the gentle rasp of his teeth, he worshipped every beautiful, silky-smooth bit of her, top to toe, only leaving out the feminine heart of her.

He saved that for last.

And when he eased her sleek thighs apart and settled between them, she was clutching the sheets in her strong little fists, urging him onward with soft, hungry cries. By then, he couldn't wait any longer, either. He parted the dark gold curls and kissed her there, intimately. She cried out and clutched at his shoulders and moved so eagerly against his questing tongue.

He drank from her, his body aching to claim her fully, but his mind set on other pleasures, on the rich, musky taste of her, on her sweet, pleading cries, on the need to feel her shatter against his tongue. His mind spun with images of her, memories from long ago and yesterday and just that afternoon. Memories of Lili that he would always have. That even his guilt and his gut-deep knowledge that he didn't deserve her couldn't take from him.

She rose to the crest of her pleasure. He continued to kiss her. As she found the peak, he felt the sweet, delicate sensation he'd been waiting for, the butterfly-wing beating of her climax against his tongue.

Still, he kissed her. Until she went limp against the sheets and moaned and pushed at his shoulders, protesting softly, "Too much, no more. I need a moment, to catch my breath…"

He moved up her body then, pausing to dip his tongue into the well of her navel, marveling at the slightly rounder curve of her belly—hardly enough for anyone to notice yet.

But *he* noticed. There was nothing about her that he didn't see, didn't know, didn't claim. Now was his chance, at last, to touch her, to kiss her, to catalog her perfections. He didn't want to miss a millimeter of her. For this magical moment in time, he could pretend she was his forever.

And when the real world claimed them again, he would have new memories, a treasure chest of them, to open in the dark heart of the lonely night. To keep him company in all his solitary days to come.

He gathered her close, turning her and himself, so they lay facing each other. He smoothed her hair. She stroked his shoulder, her rapid breathing slowing now, the hot pink blush on her cheeks and breasts slowly fading, leaving a trace of redness from his day-old beard.

"Oh, Alex," she said in a breathless whisper. "We should always be like this...."

He combed her hair with his fingers, petted her cheek with the back of his hand. "Stubble burn. Sorry..."

She caught his fingers, kissed them. "It's nothing. It was worth it. Very much worth it." She dipped her head closer, kissed him so sweetly. "Wonderful." She kissed the word onto his mouth. "And we aren't even close to finished yet. In fact, we are just getting started."

"You have plans?" He traced the full, luscious shape of her lips with his tongue.

"I have...designs," she said, kissing the words onto his mouth.

"Designs?" He was aching to have her. But it was a good ache, one he could easily bear, one that, tonight, at last, he knew would be fully satisfied.

"Designs on *you,*" she explained, her lips still brushing his, her little hand busy between them, tracing the long scar that ran from his left shoulder diagonally across to a point under his right arm. "Designs on your body. I love your body. Did you know that?"

"I'm very pleased to hear it, as I adore *your* body." He sucked her lower lip into his mouth, scraped it lightly with his teeth. "This could be good."

She sighed. "Oh, it could be much, much better than merely good."

"Show me, Lili." It came out on a rough rasp of breath.

She smiled her sweetest smile against his mouth. "Yes, Alex. I do believe I will." Her hand brushed his neck, caressed his chest, moving downward. She rubbed his belly, a low, purring sound coming from deep in her throat.

And then she went lower. Her smooth, cool fingers encircled him. The sensation was exquisite.

He closed his eyes, swallowed a groan, ordered his starved, too-eager manhood not to lose it, to hold out. Hold on.

And that was before she started to stroke him, before she pushed him over onto his back and rose up above him, golden and glorious in the soft candlelight. Before she bent close, her hair falling all around him, brushing his chest, his belly, his arms, falling like a thousand silk feathers along the side of his hip, making a spun-gold veil to cover him, a web of silk to hold him.

That was before her wet, hot mouth encircled him and her little hand held him in place, before her clever tongue explored him and she began to gently, insistently draw on him. To slide up and down on him, taking him in all the way and then, slowly, so slowly, letting him out—only to lower that impossibly sweet, hot mouth around him all over again.

It was heaven. It was torture. It was a perfect, agonizing, painful, delicious combination of both.

He didn't last long. How could he?

Too soon, he had to act. He took her slim shoulders, pulling her up to him, claiming her mouth as he eased her beneath him and settled himself against her, between her thighs, where he wanted, needed, *had* to be.

She opened for him, wrapping those smooth, slim legs around him, pulling him down to her, down to where she wanted him.

Which was exactly where he wanted, needed, *had* to be.

Her fingers found him again. She encircled him, guiding him, taking him into the fine, giving heat at the wet, slick heart of her womanhood.

He sank into her, drowning, surrounded, caressed. Completely lost. And only too happy to be so.

She lifted her body, enfolding him. Her soft arms held him and her sweet hips rocked him. There was no woman, ever, in the whole world like her. Not for him.

There never had been. He knew that now.

He groaned and he gave himself up to her, gave himself over to her, as he had that first time, to his everlasting shame. She was the promise he'd been running from since they were children, the hope he'd denied, the truth he'd turned away from, the road back he couldn't yet allow himself to see.

She was more than he could deal with, more than he'd bargained for, more than he knew how to handle or control. Without hesitation, she claimed him and there was no part of him she didn't own, didn't hold so tenderly, didn't rock into sweetest, hottest oblivion.

She gave him everything. More than he'd ever dared to imagine. More, much more, than he could ever hope to deserve.

For now, he gave in to her. He let her take him, let her sweep him away. Let her take him up, soaring. She was the finest, highest, truest wave. Way out on the open sea. She curved above him, tenderly, closing over him, crashing down upon him. She took him under, took him with her.

Gasping, ecstatic, he called her name.

"Alex?"

He opened his eyes to darkness. For a moment, he was in the ground, swallowed by it. In that hole they kept him in during the last year of his captivity. Panic clawed at him. Sweat bloomed on his skin.

"Alex?" Lili's voice. Soft. Soothing, in the darkness. Her small hand in his, holding on. Holding *him*.

And he remembered. All of it. Devon was dead. And he had escaped. And there was Lili: his wife.

He remembered his cruelty to her—his many cruelties. And their honeymoon. And that night on the water. The storm.

The island, the little stone house...

And the two of them together.

For now.

He turned to her. How could he help himself? Even in the darkness, she brought light. Warmth.

The impossibility that was hope.

The hope he kept denying over and over. The hope she kept offering, like a cool drink of water in an endless desert, like a ray of light in the deepest, darkest place. Even in a room with no windows, it didn't matter. Wherever she was, she brought light.

Her sweet breath across his cheek. A millimeter, two—yes. Contact. Her mouth melting into his, a perfect fit. He kissed her, slowly. Deeply. She made a small, tender sound. He drank in that sound.

And then her hands were there, touching him, brushing the sides of his throat, cradling his face, her fingers against his beard-scratchy cheeks, her palms under his chin. "Alex. I'm so glad. To be here with you. Like this."

So am I. The words were there, pushing to get out. He didn't let them. He had no right to let them.

She whispered, "I know I shouldn't be glad. It's selfish to be so happy here, alone with you. Selfish when I know that the people who care for us are desperately searching, hoping against hope that we're still among the living, that they will find us, somehow, and bring us home safe...."

His heart, that dark place he had for so long thought empty and cold—it ached. He couldn't bear to hear more. "Shh." He moved his head on the pillow, close again, so he could breathe the hushing sound against her parted lips. "Shh..."

She shook her head, her lips brushing his again, back and forth. "No, not yet. There's more. I know that you don't want to hear me, but you *will* hear me."

"Don't..."

She wouldn't listen. "I know you, Alex. I know what

you're doing. I know you're…allowing yourself this time with me. But that you will somehow make yourself pay."

"Stop."

She didn't. "Don't you see? It's no good. You make yourself pay for every moment of happiness, every taste of pleasure—and that means *I* pay, too. And the baby. Oh, Alex. Think about her."

He wanted to grab her close and kiss her senseless. He wanted to push her away, roll from the bed and run out the door. Somehow, he managed to do neither. "The baby will have *you*," he said. "The baby will be fine."

"The baby needs her father. And *I* need you, Alex. I need you beside me, not just for tonight, for all the nights. We can do so much in the world together. If only you will forgive yourself for whatever it is you feel you have to suffer for. If only you will see that forgiveness *is* waiting for you. You only have to reach out and claim it."

"Lili, let it go."

She made a sound that was something like a sob. "Let it go? How can you say that? This is your life we're talking about. And my life. And the life of our child."

"Lili…"

"Oh, Alex." A long sigh escaped her. "Sometimes you make me so very, very tired."

He thought about losing her. How he would have to do that again. He couldn't bear it, to think it. Not now. He wanted the feel of her. He wanted forgetfulness. Just for a little while. "Kiss me."

"It won't solve anything."

"I know, Lili. Kiss me…."

She obeyed. She pressed her lips to his, at first with reluctance. But then with a soft-sighing, eager willingness. The kiss was long and deep and sweet.

And the moment he dared to lift his mouth from hers, she

started in again. "Did you ever stop to think that the two of us, you and me, we've been bound together since we were children?"

"All the time," he confessed. Why not be honest, here at least, alone with her on this nameless island in the darkness of the middle of the night?

"Why were you always so cruel to me?"

How to tell her? "I thought I had so many important things to do." He gave a low laugh, one that was totally lacking in humor. "And you would keep me from them, ensnare me, seduce me from my purpose. You would be a queen and I would be merely your consort. I thought that would never be enough for me."

"Ah, I see that." She was smiling. He could hear it in her voice. Leave it to Lili to smile when he told her how petty and small-hearted he'd been.

He went on. "I belittled you."

"You certainly did."

"I thought…if I could make you less, somehow that would set me free. Somehow, I could turn away from you and go about my life alone, unencumbered by the everyday things like marriage and family. Not bound to you or to the endless obligations of state that being your consort would entail. I could…find the truth in the world and write about it and make everyone see."

"See what, Alex?"

Ruefully, he confessed, "That's the thing. I was never sure exactly what I was going to make the world see. But I knew that when I finally figured that little detail out, everything would fall into place."

"Ah." She laughed, low. He found himself chuckling, too. And then she said, "Alex, you should laugh more often."

He touched her hair. Spun silk. "Perhaps."

"Absolutely—and you're not telling me everything, are you?"

His gut clenched. He rolled away from her, onto his back. "I am not going to talk about Afghanistan."

"Oh, I know," she answered airily, rising up, bending over him, her hair falling across his shoulder and his chest, caressing him. He felt the quick touch of her lips against his cheek. "That's okay. You will. In time."

"You're wrong there." He said it flatly. With finality.

She only said gently, "Let's not argue about it."

"Fair enough. Let's not."

"And I wasn't referring to Afghanistan anyway," she said. "We were speaking of the past, of the reasons you were constantly pushing me away."

"Didn't I just explain all that?"

"You didn't tell me all of it. Only the parts that make you look the worst. I think there's more. I think there was some… nobility in your cruel behavior back then. Misguided nobility. But nobility, nonetheless."

"No, there wasn't."

"I know there was. At least a little…"

"No. No nobility. None." He stared blindly up at the darkness, all too aware of the living warmth of her so close, the slight weight of her arm across his belly, the wonderful scent of her, lavender and woman.

"Ah, well. I suppose we shall have to agree to disagree on the subject of your nobility." She laid her head down on his chest. "I would actually have married Rule if he hadn't finally followed his heart and found Sydney. I really had myself convinced that I was in love with him."

He couldn't stop himself. He stroked her hair. "Rule is a fine man."

"Yes. And it would have been a disaster if I had married him. He never loved me as a woman, only as his honorary little sister. And I…I didn't love him either—not as a woman loves a man. But I was too naive to see that then. Plus, I had my mind set on Rule. I'm a little ashamed of myself, of how purposely blind I was when it came to him. I was staying in Montedoro, at the Prince's Palace, for weeks on end, making a pest of myself, just waiting. So certain that any day he would knock on my door, drop to his knees and propose to me. I was…so hungry, Alex. For love. So full of dreams and hope."

"Innocent," he whispered. He pressed his lips to her fragrant hair. "You were innocent. And I can see why you were set on Rule. I thought it was the right thing, too, you and Rule. He's kind and good. So charming. And patient and thoughtful. All the things I never was."

"So you *were* being noble. At least a little—stepping aside for Rule."

"How could I step aside? I wasn't in the running. I was the last man you would have considered. And I honestly believed I wanted it that way."

"But then…" She let the words trail off, an invitation for him to continue.

And he surprised himself. He *did* continue. "That day in April, at the palace, when I found you sobbing on your knees outside my rooms? You told me that Rule had married another. And for a moment, a split second, I was glad. Fiercely glad. And then, instantly, I was angry. At you. At myself. At Rule for marrying someone who wasn't you and making me feel glad about it. I insulted you. And you tried to slap me. And when I caught your wrist to stop you…" He didn't go on. He couldn't. He'd already said too much.

Way too much.

"Oh, Alex," she whispered. He gritted his teeth and waited for her to start chattering away, analyzing him and his actions, urging him to go on, to tell her more. But then she pressed her warm, full lips to his chest, laid her head back down over his heart and softly whispered, "It's all right."

No, it wasn't. It wasn't all right. Not in the least. "What I did was unforgivable. I took advantage of you when you were at your most vulnerable. There is no excuse for what I did that day."

She laughed. "Please. You would have stopped in an instant. We both know that. All I had to do was tell you no."

"It's not that simple. Don't make excuses for me. The bald truth is that I seduced you."

"I don't know what it is with you, Alex. You have some obsession with casting yourself as the villain. You are not the villain. I'm twenty-six years old. And I am more than capable of saying no. But I didn't *want* to say no. I wanted exactly what happened. I wanted *you*."

"You were in no position to know what you wanted. You were an innocent, a virgin."

"Yes, I was. I didn't realize it at the time, but I see now that I was saving myself. For you, as it turned out."

He chuckled again. He couldn't help it. "Did you ever meet a lemon you couldn't turn to lemonade?"

"Never. Not one."

He held her closer, kissed the top of her foolish, beautiful head. "In your heart, you're *still* an innocent."

"I look on the bright side. It's a choice, Alex."

He didn't argue. Why waste his breath? He wasn't about to change her mind. And as long as he was being painfully honest, he had to admit that he didn't want to change her mind—or anything about her. She was perfect just as she was.

She lifted up away from him.

He caught her silky shoulder. "Stay here." He pulled her close again, speared his fingers into her hair, capturing her face between his two hands. "Kiss me."

"Oh, Alex…"

He pulled her down to him. She didn't object. Sighing, she covered his mouth with hers. She opened, let him into her sweetness, met his tongue with hers. He tasted her deeply, his hand straying downward to cup her mound, to comb the short, sweet curls there, to part them, part *her*.

Already, she was wet for him. She moaned into his mouth. Still kissing him, she lifted onto her knees. He felt her bring one leg across him, straddling him. Her hair slid over him, down the sides of his neck, against his chest....

He kissed her some more, his fingers stroking her, finding the bud of her greatest pleasure, teasing it until she cried out and reached down between them. She took him in her hand. And she guided him home.

Slowly, so slowly, she lowered her body onto him. He thought he would die, it felt so good. So right...

When she had him, when she owned him, she began to move. It was all he could do just to hold on. He clasped her sweet, round bottom in his hands and he went with her, went where she took him.

All the way to heaven.

At the end, she sat up, braced her hands on his chest and pressed down on him, taking him even deeper than before. He felt her completion, felt it take form, felt her body contracting around him.

That did it. He couldn't hold out any longer. He went over the edge of the universe with her. Surging up into her, he reached up through the darkness and found her. He pulled her down to him, found her sweet mouth again and buried his hands in her tangled hair.

At the very last, she broke the kiss. He opened his eyes, seeking hers, finding only the night, but knowing that she was there, warm and soft and beautiful, hovering above him.

She whispered, breathless, her hips still moving on him. "I love you, Alex. Love you, love you. Always. Love you…"

He didn't answer. He had no right to answer. He only pulled her down again and silenced her with another kiss.

Chapter Eleven

The next day, they saw no boats. The clear, blue sky brought no helicopters bearing Alex's specially trained men to rescue them.

Still, it was a beautiful day. A happy day. Lili tried not to think of her father, of Alex's family, of everyone worried sick about them, trying desperately to find them. Instead, she focused on this precious time with her husband, on the joy of just being with him.

Because it was a joy. Here, on "their" island, as she had already come to think of it, he was like a different person. He smiled at her often. He teased her, playfully. In fun. He even laughed out loud now and then.

No, he didn't return the words of love she'd lavished on him the night before. But she had to remember that he *was* Alex. He never had been good at happiness. And Rome wasn't built in a day.

They went fishing together—or rather, Lili went with

Alex. He did the fishing. And she made him clean what he caught. It was a messy, smelly job, just as he'd warned her it would be. He said she should learn to fish and to clean her catch.

She held firm. "I've fished before. If I ever *have* to, I can do it. And I saw how you cleaned them. I could manage that, too. If I had to. But I don't. Because you can do it."

The little goat, which had followed them down to the beach, said, "Maa, maa."

Lili granted her an approving nod. "See, even the goat agrees with me."

Alex only grunted and dropped his line back in the water.

Later, back at the little house, Lili cooked the fish. They turned out quite well, actually. Alex praised her cooking skills.

Even better, once the meal was done, he pulled her onto his lap and kissed her. His rough beard scratched her face and she didn't care in the least. She kissed him back with enthusiasm.

The kissing led where kisses often lead. They went to bed early, but not to sleep. She relished every kiss he gave her, every tender, arousing caress. She wished that somehow they could be rescued *and* that he would continue to be the open, loving man she held in her arms that night.

The next day was much the same as the one before it. Alex did some fishing, catching enough for their evening meal. They also made a circuit of the island, checking on the driftwood messages and the readiness of the signal fires. Two planes flew by, far overhead, vanishing much too quickly. Alex used the last two flares trying to get their attention, but to no avail. They saw one boat—far out, a tiny dot on the horizon. And they were near a signal fire at the time. They set it ablaze.

The boat never got closer. It only seemed to get smaller and smaller until it vanished from sight.

That night, Alex talked of reinflating the raft, of paddling out far enough that maybe he would sight another island. He spoke in the singular, which meant he didn't plan to take her with him. He expected her to remain there, out of harm's way on the island, while he took all the chances.

She thought of the tricky currents out beyond the safety of the cove, of the sudden storm that had overturned the *Lady Jane*. "That could be dangerous. And in any case, if you're going, I'm going with you."

"No. There's the baby to think of. You'll stay here—you and the baby, where it's safe."

She hated that he had a point. She did want to keep their baby safe. But if he did end up going, she didn't think she could stand to remain behind.

Why get into that argument when she didn't have to, though? She could fight that battle if and when she had no choice. For now, she tried a different angle. "You could stay here, too. We might as well all three be safe."

"We can't just wait here, doing nothing, forever."

She didn't see why they couldn't do exactly that. "Your men are well-trained and methodical. Eventually, they will find us."

"Yes, but how long will it take?"

"Someone will come, Alex."

He only looked at her, that distant look of his, the one that told her she was getting nowhere with him on this subject. And she did understand his impatience.

Because she understood *him*.

He'd done all he could to prepare, to be ready to signal any boat or aircraft that might come close enough to spot them. He was growing tired of waiting for something to happen.

Time chafed at him. He wanted action, a swift resolution to what he viewed as their plight.

She gave up arguing with him and bargained instead. "Wait a few more days at least. Please, Alex."

He blew out a hard breath. "Three days. All right," he agreed. "Then I'm going to try it."

"Three *full* days. Then on the fourth day, if you really feel you must…"

He glowered. "That's four damn days."

"Alex. Please."

"I don't understand this. My men should have found us by now. And not only my men. Your father will have mobilized an army of searchers. And my family will have done the same."

"We have no idea how far the storm pushed us after we lost radio contact, or how far we drifted overnight. And there are more than a thousand islands off Croatia. You've got to give them a little time."

"Four more days is too long."

"Think of it this way. In four days, it will still be less than a week that we've been marooned here. And it's not four days. It's three days."

"Not the way I count it."

She asked again, "Wait till the fourth day? Please?"

Finally, reluctantly, he gave in. "All right. The fourth day. And then I'm going."

The next day passed. And the one after that. Alex remained kind and attentive. But she could feel his distraction, his focus on the world out there beyond the small paradise they had made on the island together. He was so certain they should have been rescued by now and unwilling to just let it go and enjoy himself in the time they had left here. Instead, he prowled the island, his gaze on the horizon. He scanned the sky, willing their rescuers to hurry up and find them.

Lili went with him in the mornings of those two days. But in the afternoons, she stayed at the stone house. She performed the simple chores required to keep the place in order. And she had found a box of tattered paperbacks under the bed. Some were in Italian, which she could read with effort, but most were in English. There were detective novels and some Westerns, a couple of juicy romances and several self-help books. When she finished her few housekeeping duties, she would grab a book and stretch out on the bed.

It was lovely and relaxing, life on the island. Plus, there were the nights. Every night, she and Alex made slow, beautiful love and then she slept curled up close against him. When they were in bed, she kept him busy enough that he wasted none of his energy worrying about when rescue would finally come. She gave him no chance to indulge his impatience for the time to pass, for the day to come when he could finally take action and row out to the open sea.

The next day dawned, the third day after they'd made their agreement, the final day before he would insist he was taking the raft and rowing out to search for another island nearby. Lili tried not to think about tomorrow, about all the dangerous things that might happen in a raft out on the open water, about the fight they would have when she insisted that if he was going, so was she.

But by then, worry had started to drag on her. She sent more than one beseeching prayer heavenward, that rescue would come that day or early the next. Soon. Before Alex had a chance to take the raft out to sea.

That night, they made love for hours. Lili never wanted to stop. It almost seemed to her that if she could only keep kissing him, keep touching him, keep holding him deep within her, the morning would never come. He would never have to take the raft out. They could make the night last forever.

But eventually, sleep claimed her. One moment she was

resting with her head on his shoulder, planning to lift up on an elbow and start kissing him again—and the next moment her heavy eyelids were lowering of their own accord.

"Sleep," he whispered. She felt his lips against her forehead, the lovely roughness of his beard.

She gave in. She let her eyes drift shut.

She woke suddenly.

It was still dark. They'd left the bedroom window open. She turned her head on the pillow. Outside, it seemed to her that the sky was paling, that dawn must be near.

The goat was crying, "Maa, maa, maa...."

"Alex?" She reached for him, but he wasn't there. His side of the bed was still warm. She sat up and squinted through the dimness toward the open door to the dressing room and the bathroom beyond. He was probably in there.

The goat kept on crying. "Maa, maa..."

And then she heard it: scuffling. And grunting sounds. The sounds were coming from outside. She got up, went to the window, looked out.

But all she saw was the deserted side yard. The grunting and scuffling were coming from around by the back door.

And judging by the fact that Alex hadn't sprinted in from the other room to investigate the odd noises, he was probably out there *making* those noises. Or *helping* to make them. Because it sounded to her like a fight was going on out there.

"Maa, maa, maa..." The little goat kept crying.

Pausing only to scoop up the old nightgown and pull it on, Lili grabbed the survival kit flashlight from the table by the bed and raced out to the kitchen. The shutters were open in there, too. She could see that the back door was slightly ajar. And she could hear the scuffling and grunting continuing from outside.

She needed a weapon of some sort. The flashlight was

thin and lightweight. It wouldn't do. Frantically, she tried to decide what to use.

"Maa, maa, maa!"

Someone grunted really loudly and something heavy fell against the side of the house.

A kitchen knife? Oh, she really didn't like the idea of having to stab anybody. So she hefted the big iron frying pan she used for cooking fish and she raced for the door, slowing when she got there, easing through it, trying not to make a sound.

Outside, it seemed lighter. To the east, the gleam on the horizon told her the sun was coming up.

"Maa, maa, maa!" The little goat came racing toward her from around the corner of the house. She backed up against the wall by the door and peeked around to where the grunting was coming from.

She saw two men fighting. One of them, the big one, was naked. That would be Alex. She dropped the flashlight, lifted the frying pan high with both hands and waded in to bop the other smaller man on the head.

But then Alex said, "Lili, put that pan down. Can't you see, I've got him?" She paused, peering closer and saw that Alex had the other guy's hand wrenched up behind his back and one powerful arm locked around his neck.

"Ugh, gnuh, aggh," said the other man, trying to break free of Alex's grip.

"Stop struggling," Alex said to the other man. And then he must have wrenched the man's hand farther up his back, because the man let out a groan of real pain.

Lili lowered the frying pan. "Alex, you're hurting him…."

Alex sent her a look. Even through the gloom of very early morning, she read that look. "I'm doing the best I can here, Lili." He said something else to the stranger in his grip. Lili didn't understand the words that time, but she recognized the language: Croatian.

The man grunted and nodded.

Alex said something else.

The man nodded again. Alex must have loosened his hold around the poor fellow's throat because the man managed to croak out, "All right."

Alex asked, "You speak English?"

"Damn right."

"You have a name?"

The man said, "I'm Jack Spanner. And this is my bloody house."

The next few minutes were a bit awkward.

Alex was reluctant to let go of Jack, who was clearly unhappy about being jumped at the back door of his own home. They stood outside as the sun rose, Alex, without a stitch on, holding Jack's arm behind his back—but a bit more gently now.

Lili said, "Alex, surely you can see that Jack has a right to be annoyed."

Alex grunted. "That's what I'm worried about."

She suggested, "If you let go of him, I'm sure he'll behave. Won't you, Jack?"

Before Jack could reply, Alex grunted again. "Why should I believe him, whatever he says?"

Jack said. "You attacked *me*."

"I heard you creeping around out here. What did you expect?"

"It's my bloody house!"

Lili explained, "Our boat capsized in a storm. We drifted here on a life raft six days ago. We're sorry we broke into your house, but we didn't really have much choice."

Jack said, "I saw the bonfire you laid on the beach. And

your names, too, written in driftwood and stones. Lili and Alex…"

"Yes. Um. Ahem. That's us. Lovely to meet you, Jack," Lili said. Alex said nothing. He still held Jack from behind.

Jack asked cautiously, "Just the two of you, then?"

"And the goat," she said, trying to lighten the mood a little.

Jack was not amused. "That's Bianka, one of Marina's goats—where are the others?"

"Well, if there were other goats, they're gone now."

"And what about the chickens? Have you slaughtered the chickens? And what in bloody hell have you done with Marina?"

"We haven't seen any chickens." Lili thought of the envelope with Jack's name on it that still waited on the kitchen table. Apparently, it did not hold good news for Jack. "Just the one goat. And no other people, until you. The house was locked up tight when we got here." She sent her naked husband a hopeful glance. "Alex, perhaps if we could all go inside?"

Finally, after a brief negotiation during which Alex implied dire harm to Jack should he try to make more trouble and Jack insisted that *he* was not the one making the trouble in the first place, Alex released Jack and the three of them went inside.

Alex went straight to the envelope propped against the blue pitcher. "I think this is for you."

Jack glared. "You been reading my private mail?"

"No. That envelope was propped against that blue pitcher when we got here. Neither of us has opened it."

Still frowning, Jack took it, folded back the flap and removed a single sheet of paper.

Alex asked Lili, "Get me my pants?"

She had a contrary urge to tell him to go get them himself, but then she realized he was only being cautious. He didn't yet want to let the newcomer out of his sight. "More than happy to, darling," she answered sweetly. She popped back into the bedroom, grabbed his cargoes off the floor and brought them back to him.

By that time, Jack had wadded up the sheet of paper in a white-knuckled fist and lowered himself to a chair. "She's left me," he said in a desolate whisper. "Says she's had enough of being alone. She took the chickens and the goats and went back to her father's farm on the mainland."

"Maa, maa, maa." The white goat had eased her nose in the unlatched door. Alex strode over there, pushed the intruding nose back out and shut the door.

"Except for Bianka." Jack held up the fisted paper. "Marina says here she couldn't catch her."

"Rough break, man," said Alex.

"She has a cell phone," Jack complained. "She could have called me and told me what she was planning. But no. She leaves me a note—and she refuses to answer the phone when I call. I was afraid something had happened to her."

Lili begged to differ. "Not that afraid," she chided. "Your Marina has been gone for a week at least. And there's no fuel to run the generator, so it's possible her cell was dead and she *couldn't* call you—not until she got off the island, anyway. And by then, I'll venture a guess, she had decided she *wouldn't* call you."

"It's that mother of hers," Jack muttered darkly. "Always popping over to see how her baby girl is doing, filling Marina's head with lies about me."

"At least her mother came to check on her."

Jack's shoulders slumped. "You've a point, I must admit it. I only thought she was giving me a big dose of the silent treatment."

"You should have come back sooner," Lili scolded.

"Give the poor man a break," said Alex.

"The poor man? Marina's the one who suffered, left here on her own for Lord knows how long with only chickens and goats for company—go after her," she urged, making shooing motions at Jack with both hands. "Get her back. And next time, don't be gone for so long."

Both men rolled their eyes. Jack said, "I'm a fisherman. I have to work. That means I'm off for days on the boat. Marina knew that when she married me. She said she loved her time alone."

Lili suggested the obvious. "Perhaps it was more time alone than she had bargained for. Make some changes. It can't be that difficult."

Now both men groaned. Alex said, "It's just like a woman. They marry a man and then set about trying to make him into someone else."

She couldn't resist reminding them both, "Some men could use a little improving—some men could use a *lot*." And then before either man could argue with her further, she turned, went into the bedroom and quietly shut the door.

Alex stared after her. "Lili's a woman of definite opinions. Always has been."

"Aren't they all?" Jack set the rumpled letter on the table and smoothed it with his palms. "And she may have a point or two," he admitted grudgingly. "I get working trying to fill my tanks, I lose track of the days...."

"You're not Croatian by birth, are you?"

Jack shook his head. "Came on holiday, decided to stay. I *was* born a fisherman, though. Bought me boat eight years ago now."

"Sorry we took over your house—*and* about that scrap we got into. You know how it goes."

Jack agreed. "A man can't be too careful." Alex offered

his hand. Jack took it. "No harm done. Glad the place was here when you needed it."

Alex dropped into the other chair. "You came in your fishing boat, then?"

Jack nodded. "She's in the western cove. Be happy to take you to Korčula." Korčula was one of the larger of the southern islands off Croatia. It was also the second most populated, after the northern island of Krk. Jack went on, "Korčula's not far and I have to return there anyway to pick up my crew. From there, you can catch a ferry to the mainland."

How strange, Alex found himself thinking. All the days of waiting and wondering, worrying no one would ever come for them.

And then, just like that, they were rescued. Now he wouldn't have to fight with Lili over whether she was going with him when he took the raft out. He wouldn't have to risk going out there himself into the deep waters beyond the cove.

They would return home now. Everything would go back to the way it had been before.

He remembered what he had promised himself when he'd allowed himself to let down his guard with Lili. That when they were rescued, when they were safely home, he would withdraw again and reclaim his solitary life as it had been before.

Already, he missed what he and Lili had found here. He hated to lose it.

And why should you lose it? He could almost hear Lili lecturing him now.

She would insist that they didn't have to lose anything. He almost smiled thinking of the things that Lili would say when he tried to withdraw from her, of the arguments she would lay out for why they should continue as they had been here on the island, where they had only each other. Where he had finally been forced to realize what a truly fine woman she was.

Where she had said she loved him and then set about proving it in a thousand different ways.

Where they had been happy.

Together.

Happy. Imagine that. He was not supposed to be happy. He'd convinced himself that he couldn't be happy ever. Not after what had happened, not after the evil he had caused.

But the clear fact was, he *had* been happy here with Lili. And the idea of turning his back on her now, of pushing her away and then keeping her at a distance, of sleeping without her curled close to his side...

It all felt alien to him now. Pointless. As though he wasn't the same man he had been just a week ago. And the things that had seemed so real to that other man, that man he had been just a week ago...they had no meaning to him now.

Jack said, "You still with me, mate?"

Alex shook himself. "Right here. Sorry. Just thinking. I wonder..."

"Spit it out."

"All I really need is to make a call and we can be picked up right here on the island. You wouldn't happen to have a working cell on you, would you?"

"Course I do." Jack reached in his pocket and pulled out a phone. "I never go anywhere without me phone."

Chapter Twelve

A few minutes later, Lili emerged from the bedroom, fully dressed. By then, Alex had already made the call that would bring rescue.

The helicopter from the *Princess Royale,* piloted by one of Alex's best men, would be touching down near the stone house within the hour. As it happened, the search had moved into the area. Alex's men would no doubt have spotted the driftwood messages and come for them that day or the next day at the latest.

Lili was just grateful that Jack had appeared before Alex insisted on going off on the raft. In this case, timing was everything. They could have been lost all over again, and just before they would have been found.

She didn't remind Alex of that. She had a feeling, from the sheepish look in his eyes, that he already knew it.

Lili brewed tea and opened a tin of cookies. Alex went to

the bedroom to finish dressing and gather up their things. That gave her a few minutes alone with Jack.

"Take a break from fishing and go get your wife." She took Jack's weathered hand and tucked her big wad of kunas into his rope-scarred palm.

Jack had his pride. "That's a lot of money. Too much." He tried to give it back to her.

She only leaned back and put up both hands. "Believe me, I can get along without it. But you need Marina. And I have a feeling she needs you."

Finally, Jack agreed to go and try to work things out with his wife. He also promised he would take good care of Bianka.

"See that you do," Lili replied. "I love that goat."

Jack said regretfully, "I would give her to you...."

Lili smiled. "But Marina loves her, too."

"How did you know?"

"Just a guess." She leaned close and kissed his cheek. "I've been meaning to ask where you got your Cadillac."

"It was here when I bought the place."

"Does it run?"

"Of course. Marina and I used to drive it round the island." Jack's eyes got a faraway look. "She loved that, riding in the Cadillac, with the top down. I haven't had time to drive her around lately, though."

"Make time."

"I'll try."

"You know Montedoro, Jack?"

"I know it. Where the nobs go. I seen pictures of the Prince's Palace and that big casino at Colline d'Ambre."

"How about Alagonia?"

"Off the coast of Spain. A beautiful little piece of real estate."

"Alex is from Montedoro. I'm an Alagonian."

"Hold on." Jack had paled a bit. "When I dropped my crew off on Korčula, I saw the papers. A missing prince and princess, lost somewhere in the Dalmatians..."

Lili nodded. "And you, Jack, have saved us."

"You kissed my cheek," Jack muttered in disbelief. "I seen the prince in the altogether, and got into a right fine scrap with him as well. He shook me hand...."

Lili said softly, "There will be a reward. It will be a large one."

"But..." He held up the money she'd already given him. "This'll more than do it, Your Grace."

"There will be a lot more."

"But all I did was to come home."

"And you should come home more often. Spend a little more time with Marina. Promise me."

Jack touched his cheek where she'd kissed him. "Your Majesty, if she'll have me back, I swear to you, I will."

They were ready well before the helicopter came. There hadn't been much to prepare. Lili had her pack. Alex had told Jack where to find the raft and given him the survival pack to go with it. Jack promised to store them both on his boat. They might come in handy one day.

Just before the helicopter arrived, Lili said goodbye to Bianka. She cried a little to have to leave the sweet goat behind. And then the loud beating sound of the whirring helicopter blades had Bianka scrambling for cover. Lili dried her tears and let the little goat go.

Jack stood out of the way of the blades as Lili and Alex climbed aboard.

Moments later, they were lifting into the warm, clear morning air. Lili looked down at Jack waving them off, at the stone house and the barn and the two sheds. She had been so happy there.

Always, she would remember the house and the beautiful island as a place of true enchantment, the place where she'd found her heart's desire. The place where she'd found Alex at last. Where she had discovered what it could be, to have her lifelong dream: a real marriage, a true partnership of equals.

Since April, every day had seemed like the worst day of her life. She'd given up hope, she truly had, that she would ever find the love she longed for. She, who always looked on the bright side, had truly despaired. How could she not? Tied to a man who didn't even like her, with a baby on the way. She believed that marriage was for a lifetime. And then somehow, she had allowed herself to be bound until death to a man who would never love her.

But then they went out on the *Lady Jane* and got caught in the whirlwind and ended up stranded. Being shipwrecked was the best thing that had ever happened to her.

And to Alex, too, although she couldn't be sure he would be willing to admit that. In fact, her stomach was definitely knotted with dread. Now that they were rescued, would he revert to the old Alex?

Would they end up miserable, living separate lives, barely speaking, right back where they'd started? Just the thought that he might throw it all away, turn his back on everything they had found together, put a gray cast to a bright and sunny day.

He'd damn well better not revert. If he threw their happiness away now, she was going to kill him.

She slid her hand into his. He didn't pull away. In fact, he squeezed her fingers and even leaned close to give her a quick, brushing kiss.

She smiled at him, her heart lifting. But he was already turning away to say something to the pilot.

Alex expected a hugfest when they landed on the *Princess Royale* and he expected right.

Lili's father was aboard, as were his own parents. They'd all flown to Dubrovnik and then boarded the yacht five days before, when the early searches had come to nothing.

It was a tearful reunion, but in a good way. They were all so grateful to have Alex and Lili safe again.

"We never doubted for a moment that you would be found," Lili's father said gruffly.

Overhead, helicopters hovered. And boats surrounded the *Princess* on all sides. The paparazzi were on the job, snapping away endlessly, getting shots of all of them hugging and crying, just like any ordinary family might do when two of their own came home safe after vanishing without a trace for days on end.

No one wanted to sail home on the *Princess*. That would take days. Jets were waiting in Dubrovnik, one for His Majesty and one for Her Sovereign Highness and family.

Lili insisted on a bath before she would go anywhere. "And poor Alex desperately needs a shave…." She granted him a look that dared him to disagree.

He rubbed his cheek. "My bride is right—but then, she always is."

His mother was watching him. "Alexander, I believe I sense a change in you—a change for the better."

He laughed. It felt good. "Lili has worn me down at last."

The two of them retired to their stateroom, where they cleaned up and changed into fresh clothes.

Before they rejoined the others, he took her in his arms. "You look beautiful."

She searched his face. "I'm afraid, Alex."

He kissed the tip of her nose. "Of what? We've been rescued. We're safe."

"Am I going to lose you now?" The jewel-blue eyes seemed full of worried questions.

He cradled her face and kissed her, a quick press of his lips to hers. "No, you're not going to lose me."

She took in a ragged little breath. "Promise?"

"Promise."

"You really are…better, then?"

"Better?" he asked, even though he knew exactly what she meant.

And she knew that he knew. "You know what I mean. Your mother noticed. You're different, more open. You seem ready to get beyond whatever happened to you when you were captured by the Taliban."

"Well, that's good, then, isn't it?"

She peered at him even more closely. "Yes, I think so…."

"But you still have your doubts about me, eh?"

"Alex, I didn't say that."

"You were thinking it—and it wasn't the Taliban who captured me. My captors were just plain kidnappers in it for the money. Kidnapping is big business in Afghanistan. The plan, which they hadn't thought through in any orderly way, was to ransom me."

"I thought they were terrorists…."

"No. Just street thugs who got lucky and grabbed a prince—and then had no idea what to do from there. We were unarmed and without security at the time. It was in Kabul, on a busy street. It was stupid of us. But after surviving the constant danger of the tribal areas, we made the fatal error of assuming we were reasonably safe in the capital."

"You said they took you for ransom?"

"That's right."

"But there was never a ransom demand, was there? I thought you simply…vanished."

"The thugs got cold feet when it came to the actual deal-making. They never made any demands, they simply traded us—up the line, you might say. Every time we were traded, our new captors took pictures and made videos of us—none of which they ever did anything with that I'm aware of. They beat us, interrogated us. But in the end, nobody seemed to know what to do with us. None of our captors had a network sophisticated enough to make a ransom demand of the Princess of Montedoro and to work out an executable plan to collect the money—let alone deliver the hostages. So there were more interrogations, more threats, more beatings. And sometimes, for months, there was nothing."

"Nothing?"

He shrugged. "Long stretches of time would go by during which we were simply prisoners, half-starved, losing hope. Ignored. They didn't even bother to torture us for months on end. It was after we were traded for that last time, three years into our captivity, that they killed Devon." He said the words. They tasted bad in his mouth, but they conveyed nothing of the real horror of what had happened to his friend. "More months went by. And then, finally, after all that time, after four damn years—finally, when I'd given up and knew I would die there, in a hole in the ground near the Pakistani border, there was a raid by American troops. I escaped in the confusion and managed to make my way to the Americans. They got me out."

She shivered. "I hate that you suffered. And I hate even more that you lost your friend." She asked, so gently, "You went to Princeton with him, didn't you?"

He took the question for exactly what it was: just one of many. He probably shouldn't have told her anything, should have kept his silence on the subject.

But he didn't want to keep his silence. Not anymore. Not really. Not with Lili, anyway. She honestly had changed him. Somehow, by some miracle of will and tenderness, she had done it, brought him, kicking and screaming and dragging his feet every step of the way, back into the world of the living again. He owed her. And he saw now that knowing the truth of what had happened to him was important to her; it *mattered* to her. He wanted her to have what mattered to her.

"Yes, Devon Lucas and I were at Princeton together," Alex said. "We both majored in journalism. After Princeton, he worked for an American newspaper. He became a war correspondent—first in Iraq and then in Afghanistan. I wanted to write about the Afghan opium trade, to explore the cultural and financial ramifications of opium cultivation and smuggling as a way of life. I contacted Devon. He was still in Afghanistan and he already had a network of guides and sources. He said he would help me out, take me where I needed to go. He'd been planning to go home before he heard from me. He *would* have gone home if not for me."

She was searching his face again. "You blame yourself for his death."

"I *am* to blame for his death."

"No."

"Yes. Devon stayed in Afghanistan because I asked him to. He was kidnapped because he was with me. When we tried to escape, they beat me, but they cut off Devon's hand."

She swallowed. Hard. "Oh, my sweet God…"

He nodded. "I had 'value' to them because I was a prince and they still believed they would find a way to demand and get a big ransom for me. Devon's only value to them was as a way to control me. And in the end, when they killed him, they did it to break me. They brought us both up out of the hole they kept us in and they shot him in the head in front of me."

Her eyes were turbulent, swirling with outrage and sadness combined. "It was *their* fault. Those thugs who took you, traded you, tortured you. *They* are the ones to blame, Alex, not you."

"Well, they paid—at least the men who shot Devon paid. They all died in the American raid."

"Good. They deserved to die."

"Lili." He smoothed her gleaming, freshly shampooed hair. "I believe you have a bloodthirsty side."

Staunchly, her blue eyes glittering now, she repeated, "They deserved to die. And it wasn't your fault."

There was no point in arguing with her over it. He told her tenderly, "I mean it. I'm all right."

She almost smiled. "You realize what a big step you've just taken?"

"Oh, have I?"

"Yes. You've finally talked to me about the things you always refused ever to talk about, about your friend Devon, about the evil men who kidnapped you, about the terrible brutality you suffered while you were a prisoner...."

"See? I'm a changed man. All because of you." He said it teasingly, even though it was true.

She studied him. "You *have* come a long way."

"Yes, I have."

And then she frowned. "But I still have this strange feeling that you're holding back something important."

He caressed her cheek and reassured her again, "I'm all right, Lili."

She sighed then. "I don't think I could bear it if you turned away from me now. That would be too impossibly cruel of you, to show me what it could be for us. And then to take it away."

"I won't turn away from you." He said the words and then wondered at them. Somehow, even though he meant them, they seemed…not quite true. She'd given him hope again, made him see that there might still be a good and productive life ahead for him. But now that the fog of self-blame and numbness had cleared, he saw not only what might be for them, as a woman and a man, a wife and her husband, a queen and her prince. He also saw what he *hadn't* done, the promises he hadn't kept. He had to fulfill those promises before he could give himself completely to the future, to Lili, and to their child.

She said, "You won't mind so much, then, being my consort, being the husband of a queen?"

"No, Lili, I won't mind that at all. It's become something of a habit for me—to be married to you. A good habit. One I'm finding I don't want to give up."

She caught his fingers, opened them, pressed them against her cool, velvety cheek and then turned her head a little so she could kiss the center of his palm. "Thank you. I needed to hear that. It's been…like a miracle for me. Our disaster of marriage somehow turning into the kind of union I've dreamed of my whole life long. I love you, Alex."

He wanted to answer in kind, but he knew he had yet to earn the right to speak to her of love. So he kissed her instead, a long kiss that, as always with Lili, only left him wanting more.

At the airport in Dubrovnik, Leo wanted Lili to return to Alagonia with him. She hugged him and kissed him again and said that she and Alex would be home to see him soon. But for now, she was going to Montedoro with her husband.

Surprisingly, Leo didn't argue or bluster or insist she do things the way he wanted them done. He kissed her again and told her he loved her. He even shook Alex's hand and commanded him to "Take good care of my little love."

Alex promised that he would. Leo boarded his royal jet

with only his attendants for company. A few minutes later, Alex and Lili were taking seats in the plane with his mother and father.

They spent the flight telling his parents all about the island, about the stone house and the little goat and the Cadillac in the shed. And about their inadvertent rescuer, Jack Spanner.

Actually, Lili did most of the talking. Alex sat back and listened. He admired the way she made a great story of it—a great story with a happy ending, which was the only kind of story of which his wife approved.

They were mobbed at Nice airport. There were photographers everywhere, clicking away, and reporters shouting questions. He put his arm around Lili, keeping her close at his side, while his men did their best to push the crowds back a little.

In the end, they gave in and answered a good number of the reporters' questions. Why not get it over with? The airport mob scene saved them the necessity of sitting through a formal press conference later.

They took a limousine to Montedoro, a convertible, with his men providing security in two other cars, one leading the way and the other behind. As they neared the Prince's Palace, his mother ordered the top put down. Crowds lined the streets. Lili and Alex waved and smiled as the people cheered their safe return.

Inside the palace, once they'd been greeted by the staff, the doctors were waiting. Alex got a cursory once-over and was quickly declared none the worse for wear. Lili's exam took a little longer. But in the end, the diagnosis was the same. Lili and the baby got a clean bill of health, too.

Later, there was a family dinner in his mother and father's private apartment. It was good, Alex thought, to be with his family again, to have Lili sitting next to him, safe and sound.

Each of his brothers took him aside and said how good it was to have him back in the family. He knew they meant in more ways than simply his safe return from the island. They were glad to see him finally truly coming back from the bad years in Afghanistan. His sisters made much of him—and of Lili. They were hugged and kissed and exclaimed over repeatedly.

There was a time when all the attention would have had him running for his rooms, to lock the door, to be alone. But not anymore. He could hold up under the assault of kisses and hugs just fine. He could even give out a few hugs of his own.

It was late when he and Lili finally retired to their palace apartment. Rufus, his loyal longtime retainer, was there, waiting. He welcomed them home—and then left them alone.

He held out his arms to Lili. She came to him, kissed him, a kiss so slow and perfect and sweet.

When he lifted his head at last, she asked him dreamily, "Could it be?"

"Could what be?"

"Everything. All of it. You. Me. Happiness. The two of us sharing that big bed in the other room at last?"

He asked, "Will you give me a chance to make up for our wedding night?"

She laughed. "Oh, that was awful. You, rolling in the door naked, telling me good-night—and then walking right out again."

"I'm sorry. I do mean that."

"I know that you do, that you *are*."

"Let me make it up to you."

"You already have—a week ago, in a creaky little bed in a plain stone house on our own private island." She slid a hand up to clasp his nape. He felt her gentle fingers in his hair. "However, if you would like to show me again how very happy you are to be with me…"

He took her hand from around his neck and guided it downward. She understood his intent without further coaching and traced a slow, naughty finger down the center of his chest, to his waist. And lower. He tried not to groan as she cupped her hand over him.

"I *am* happy," he said roughly.

"Oh, yes. I *feel* that you are." She chuckled, a sound that promised all manner of earthly delights.

He couldn't wait any longer. He scooped her high in his arms and carried her into the other room, the bedroom that had once been his, and then become hers and was now, at last, *theirs* in the truest sense of the word.

When he put her down on the turned-back bed, she looked up at him trustingly. "Oh, Alex. At last."

He lowered his lips to hers. She pulled him down onto the sheets with her. They shared an endless kiss.

After which he began the delightful business of undressing her. He unwrapped her slowly, like the precious gift she was. And then he touched her, caressing her until she moved, sighing, beneath his hand. When she shattered, he watched her face, drinking in the sight of her, the beauty of her, the open, giving sweetness of her.

"You have too many clothes on," she complained a few moments later. "We need to do something about that."

So she did. She undressed him, unbuttoning all the buttons, slipping off the sleeves, pulling down his trousers, getting rid of his shoes, getting rid of everything until they were both naked.

Together.

And then she reached for him. She took him into her, so deep and good and right, wrapping her arms and legs around him. He braced up on his elbows and watched her angel's face again as she moved beneath him, taking him higher.

Happiness. This was happiness. Happiness, which all his

life, even before his capture and imprisonment, had eluded him. Until now.

Until, at last, he'd surrendered to Lili. Until he'd let her into his heart.

She gave him everything. He could never repay her.

And she was not going to be happy with him when he told her that now that they had finally found each other in the truest sense, he was going to have to leave her again.

Chapter Thirteen

Lili woke to a wedge of sunlight peeking through the heavy curtains, falling across the bed.

Daylight, she thought, still half in dreamland. *We were rescued. We're at the Prince's Palace....*

She yawned and stretched out her hand to the other side of the giant bed, reaching for Alex.

He wasn't there.

Blinking sleep away, she sat up. "Alex?" And then she saw him, fully dressed in jeans, boots and a black knit shirt that clung so lovingly to the beautiful musculature of his chest. He sat in the wing chair by the window. "Alex..." She smiled at him. "What time..." She looked at the bedside clock as she started to ask. "Oh, my. Past eleven. I slept and slept."

"I've been waiting. I didn't want to wake you. You've had a rough time of it. The baby. The island. Me, most of all." He seemed so serious. His eyes spoke of his deep regard for her. And yet...

She knew something was happening here. Something she was not going to like. "What is it, Alex?"

"Lili…" His eyes. Yes. There was something about his eyes. The amber warmth had gone from them, leaving them so dark. Determined.

"Tell me," she commanded. "I mean it. What are you up to now?"

He didn't answer for a moment, only looked at her long and hard. And then finally he confessed, "I have to go away."

Her heart felt like it had somehow got stuck in a tightening vise. "Go away? No, that can't be. We've only just—"

He raised a hand, palm out. "I know. Believe me, I know. And I'm sorry. But I have…unfinished business, a responsibility I've let wait much too long while I sat in these rooms and wished I might die. I didn't die. Because of you, I lived. And now I have promises to keep."

What about your promise to me? And suddenly she knew. "Afghanistan. Your kidnappers. You can't really mean to go back there, go after them?"

He actually smiled, a dangerous, cool sort of smile. She was dead certain he was planning some murderous revenge. But then he said, "No, I leave them to heaven. And the consequences of their choices. Street thugs in Kabul tend to lead very short lives anyway. As do incompetent, sadistic al Qaeda sympathizers in the White Mountains."

"Not revenge…" A sigh of pure relief escaped her.

"No, not revenge."

"Then what is it, Alex? *What?*"

"Please try and understand…."

"How can I understand? I have no idea what you're planning."

"Devon's parents are still alive," he said. "Or they were, four and a half years ago. I have to go to them. And he had three brothers and four sisters. I owe each one of them a visit, and a helping hand should they need one."

The vise around her heart loosened a fraction. Of course. He would feel responsible. She could understand that completely. "Ah. Well, all right, then. They're all in America?"

"I believe so. It may take some looking, but I will find them."

"Well, then…" She tried a smile. It only trembled a little. "A trip to the States."

"Yes."

"We can go right away." She started to push back the covers.

He raised that hand again. "Lili, no."

She sank back to the pillows. "What are you telling me?"

"I need to do this alone."

Her heart rebelled. She whispered, "Alone?"

"Yes."

"Why?"

"I don't know how long it will take, how I'll be…received."

"It doesn't matter how long it takes. Or how his family reacts to you. I want to be there with you. I want to—"

"No, it's my duty and I will fulfill it. You've been through enough on my account. And there's the baby to think of."

"Alex, it's a trip to America, not an expedition into the wild. I can go with you. I *want* to go with you."

"No, I have to do it alone."

"But why?"

"Because…that's how it has to be. How I want it." He rose from the chair, so tall and strong and sternly handsome. And so completely determined to leave her.

To go somewhere in America, to be there for God only knew how long.

Her mouth felt desert-dry. She swallowed with effort, repeated too softly, "How *you* want it…"

He approached her. "Lili…"

She put up a hand. "Just…stay where you are. Oh, I am so very angry with you."

He hung his big head. "I knew you would be."

"Don't you see? We need to be together now—you and me, the baby. We're a *family* now."

"Yes, we are." He dared another step. "And we will be together. I swear it. As soon as I've done what I need to do."

She longed to grab the bedside clock and hurl it at his thick head. But instead, she fisted her hands and pressed them against her belly where their innocent child slept.

Why alone? Her heart cried. *Just tell me why you have to go alone. Why I can't go with you?*

She closed her mouth around the desperate questions. She reminded herself that of course he felt responsible for Devon's loved ones, that it was a good thing, an important step for him to go to Devon's people, to make testimony of what he knew of his friend's last years of life, to offer Devon's family his help, his support. She could even see, objectively, that he felt it was *his* responsibility and his alone, that it was something he had to accomplish on his own.

It was only, well, was this it, then? Was this their happily ever after? Alex saying goodbye and leaving for America to do what he "had to do"?

Was this what their life would be? Alex leaving. Lili left behind.

She had come to believe that he loved her, truly. In a deep, respectful, steady and also deliciously passionate way. Even if he hadn't ever managed to actually say the words.

She had *believed*. In him. In their love. After all he had put her through, she had honestly believed that they had made it work, that they were bonded together in the truest way, at last.

And now?

She didn't know what to believe now. She remembered her doubts, in their stateroom, on the *Princess Royale* the day before. She had told him straight out that she couldn't bear it if he turned away from her now.

He had promised that he wouldn't.

But what was this—his leaving her now? What was it if not turning away?

"Lili…" He said her name so tenderly. And he took the remaining steps to reach her, to bend close to her there alone in the big bed. "Lili, please…" His warm breath stirred her tangled hair. He smelled so clean and good, like everything she longed for—everything he'd seemed to give her. But now seemed bound and determined to take away all over again.

He brushed his tempting lips across her cheek. Her body ached to hold him. To be held by him.

"Just this. And that's all." He breathed the words against her skin. "Let me finish it. I need to finish it. Let me do what I can for the people Devon loved. And then, I swear to you, I will be the man you need me to be."

What else was there for her to do?

She turned toward him, accepted his tender kiss. She swallowed the tears of hurt and anger that pressed against the back of her throat. She made her mouth form something resembling a smile. "Stay safe."

He whispered her name again. Kissed her one last time. And then he was rising, turning away, striding toward the door. She pressed her lips together, ground her teeth.

She did not call him back.

After all, she had known him all her life. She knew that

dark look she'd seen in his eyes. There would be no stopping him now. He was going.

And he was going alone.

Chapter Fourteen

The days went by.

And then the weeks.

Lili kept busy with her correspondence and the occasional speaking engagement. With her work for a number of important charities. In her free time, she read some really good romances. And she painted. Scenes of light and hope and happiness.

But she was not exactly feeling the hope. Or the light or the happiness. July somehow became August. Alex didn't call. He didn't email. And he did not return.

On a Wednesday morning exactly five weeks to the day since her husband had left her, Lili stood sideways before the tall mirror in the bathroom wearing only her panties and bra. Gently, she rubbed her round belly. She was definitely showing now. Even fully dressed, one could see a definite bump.

Alex should be here to see this, see our baby growing, she thought. *Where* are *you, Alex?*

And then she caught herself. There was no sense in wishing for him, no sense in wondering where he might be now. He wasn't here. She was on her own.

Well, not completely on her own. There were people who loved her. Lots of them.

And there was her baby.

"I love you," she whispered to the tiny being within. "I love you and I will always take care of you...."

In the other room, on the bedside table, her cell phone began playing "Dancing Queen."

Alex!

Well, it could be. It *might* be....

She whirled and raced to the bedside, where she scooped up the phone and answered breathlessly, "Yes? This is Lili."

"Have lunch with me." It was Arabella. Alex's sisters were constantly at her side, keeping her company, keeping her mind off the husband she had neither seen nor heard from in a month now. She tried not to feel disappointed. Belle went on, her voice a little too bright, "We'll go down to the Triangle d'Or." The Golden Triangle was the area of exclusive shops around the world-famous Montedoran Casino d'Ambre. "We'll buy something beautiful that costs way too much. And then a slow, leisurely meal beneath a wide umbrella on a sunny patio, overlooking the sea...."

Lili couldn't help chuckling. "Listen to you, Belle. Anyone might think you were some empty-headed, self-indulgent royal instead of a hardworking professional nurse and champion of anyone in need."

"You make me sound noble indeed."

"You *are* noble."

"Lunch?"

There would be bodyguards. And they would probably be spotted by some wild-eyed paparazzo who would get right up in their faces with his cameras and demand to know where

Lili was keeping the elusive Prince Alexander. "Why don't you come to me? Rufus will fix us something nice."

"You certain you wouldn't like to splurge on Dior and Versace—and then eat out?"

"I'm sure. One o'clock?"

"I'll be there."

They sat on the shaded terrace outside the sitting room, where they could smell the sea air and feel lazy in the August heat. Belle looked wonderful, Lili thought, her thick brown hair swept up in a twist and her bronze silk blouse almost the exact color of her golden-brown eyes.

The meal was delicious as always.

Belle asked about the baby. Lili patted her stomach and said she was doing fine. Belle spoke of her brilliant American friend, Anne Benton. Anne was a single mom with a fourteen-month-old son. Belle had yet to meet the boy.

"The time just flies by." Belle shook her head. "Anne is busy with her little one, and getting her doctorate. And I'm always on my way to give a speech or off visiting a field hospital somewhere at the far end of the earth. Charlotte and I need to catch a flight to the States." Lady Charlotte Mornay was in her late forties, from an impoverished branch of the Calabretti family. She was also Belle's very capable companion and general aide-de-camp. Belle added, "I need to see my friend and meet that little boy...."

"Do it," Lili urged.

Belle nodded. "I will. Soon. I will...."

Rufus came out. He whisked away their empty plates and served them each a simple, beautiful dessert of mixed berries with mascarpone. Lili thanked him. He nodded and left them.

"Rufus takes such good care of me," Lili said.

Belle reached across the little stone table and put her hand on Lili's arm. "He's an ass. I'm going to kill him when he gets back."

Lili smiled. "Rufus?"

Belle laughed. "No, not Rufus. You *know* who I mean.... Have you called him?"

"No." Oh, she had wanted to. She had picked up the phone to do it too many times to count. But somehow, she always managed to stop herself before she finished dialing. "He has the number here. And my cell number. He knows how to reach me if he wants to talk to me—and until he *does* want to talk to me, well, what is there to say?" Lili dipped her spoon in the crystal dessert cup—and then realized she didn't feel like eating anything right at that moment. She pushed the cup away. "It really is something he *had* to do."

Belle scowled. "Don't make excuses for him."

"I'm not, believe me. I'm furious at him. All I want is for him to call—so I can hang up on him."

"He does love you. He's always loved you. We all knew it—well, my sisters and I, anyway. Because we're women and women know these things. And Damien knew, I think. And my mother and father, of course." Belle grew thoughtful. "How strange it is, really. Everyone knew but Rule. He was too busy thinking he ought to marry you himself."

"Oh, don't remind me."

"And Max was oblivious."

"Dear Max," Lili said fondly of Belle's oldest brother. "And well, I still don't see how you all could have known. *I* didn't know. And *he* certainly didn't."

Belle nodded. "Yes, let's not ever say his name again, shall we?"

"Agreed. The name leaves a bitter taste in my mouth anyway—and if you knew, well, why didn't you tell me?"

"Would you have believed me?" Belle asked.

Lili scoffed. "I would have laughed you out of the room."

Belle sipped her glass of iced mineral water. "We all knew that, too."

Lili pulled her dessert back in front of her. It was simply too beautiful to ignore. "Remember I told you about Jack Spanner, the fisherman who owned the house on the island where we were shipwrecked, the one who collected the reward for rescuing us?"

"I do remember, yes."

"Jack's wife, Marina, had left him. Before we said goodbye to Jack, I made him promise to go after her, to make it up with her."

"Did he?"

Lili beamed. "I received a lovely letter from Marina yesterday. She thanked me. She wrote that what I had said to Jack, about going after her, about staying home more, was exactly what she was trying to make him see. They're back together. Jack has promised to spend more time at home. So far, he's keeping his word."

Belle sighed. "I love it when a man finally sees the light."

"Marina said she finally realized that the only way to get her husband back was to leave him. And mean it. She had to stop telling him how unhappy she was and *show* him how it was going to be if he refused to meet her halfway."

Belle savored a bite of berries and cream. "So, when will you be leaving us?"

"I'll thank your mother today for everything. I do have the best mother-in-law on earth."

"Yes, she really is something special," Belle agreed.

"And then tomorrow I'm going home."

"Are you sure?" Adrienne asked softly. They were alone in the sitting room of her private apartment.

"No, but I'm going anyway."

"We will miss you."

"And I will miss you. I always do. When my husband returns—*if* he returns—you can tell him that I've had enough. I'm through. Finished. I've...surrendered the field."

"Lili, darling, you don't mean that."

"I'm sorry. I'm afraid I do."

"It's something you really ought to tell him yourself, don't you think?"

"I do, yes. But I haven't seen him in over a month—or heard his voice, or received one single line of correspondence—also, I have no idea where in the world he might be so that I *can* tell him myself."

"Perhaps a phone call?"

"He's the one who should call."

Adrienne suggested gently, "A letter, then?" And Lili thought of Marina's letter, left on the rough table in the little stone house. "Of course. I will leave him a letter. He might even come back and read it someday."

"He loves you. You know that?"

Lili tried a smile but failed to produce one. "He's never said so."

"He hasn't had an easy time of it."

"I know. I understand. I sincerely do. But there comes a point when a woman has to draw the line and stick by it."

"Yes. You've been a saint, darling Lili. You truly have." Her Sovereign Highness held out her arms for a goodbye hug.

Lili called her father. When she told him her husband had disappeared and she was ready to come home, she expected blustering, and at least a few vividly brutal threats against Alex's life and manly parts.

But her dear papa only said, "I will be so pleased to have you here."

He sent a jet to collect her.

She arrived at San Ferdinand Airport not far from her

country's capital city of Salvia in the late afternoon. A car, with escort, was waiting to whisk her off to D'Alagon. By some miracle of good fortune, the press had not been alerted that she was returning to Alagonia. She got off the jet and into the car without anyone firing questions at her or sticking a camera in her face.

They set out. D'Alagon was considered the royal palace of Alagonia and it was by far the largest of her father's residences. It was very old, the Gothic core of it having been built in the twelfth century, when the Castilians came to power in Alagonia. Over the endless ensuing generations, D'Alagon had been updated, enlarged and improved. It stood above the city, proud, massive, rambling, golden. D'Alagon was a fantasy blending of Gothic towers and flying buttresses, of Renaissance domes and semicircular arches, of stern, stately Baroque colonnades and the fanciful asymmetric curves and flourishes of the later Rococo style.

Lili loved D'Alagon and had always considered it her home. The first sight of it, appearing miraculously above her as the car wound its way upward, tugged at her heartstrings. It was good to be home.

If only Alex…

Lili shut her eyes. *I will not think of him.*

When she looked again, they were approaching the wide circular drive and the enormous fountain at the main entrance.

Inside, the staff was lined up and waiting. She greeted them all and then went up the right side of the wide, curving double staircase to her father's private rooms.

He was waiting in his sitting room, which was elegant and ornate, the walls covered in rich tapestries and paintings of gamboling nymphs and eighteenth-century courtiers, heavily decorated with plasterwork molded to resemble thick, twining foliage and mythical beasts. At the sight of her, he rose from a gilt-accented red velvet chair.

"My little love…"

She ran to him. "Papa!"

He wrapped his arms around her and held her close and she felt safe and cherished and surrounded by pure love. Then, of course, he *had* to mutter, "I will have his head on a pike…."

And she pulled away and told him gently, "Oh, stop it, Papa. You will do no such thing and we both know that you won't."

"A pity." He gazed down at her adoringly. "You look a bit sad, but healthy at least. And my grandson?"

She wrinkled her nose at him. "Your granddaughter is very well, thank you."

"Wonderful. And when is that wandering husband of yours coming home to you?"

"I don't know. But if he ever does, I *won't* be waiting."

"Delightful. I shall have him barred from D'Alagon."

She smiled sweetly up at him. "Yes, Papa. Please do."

Lili's cell phone rang at a little after ten that night as she was sitting in bed in her own bedroom at D'Alagon, reading an historical romance in which the heroine was a French spy and the hero an English-born pirate. It was a great book, exciting, with lots of clever dialogue and derring-do. She was totally absorbed in it.

Still, she jumped and dropped her e-reader to the coverlet when "Dancing Queen" had her cell jittering in a circle on the bedside table. She even cried out absurdly "Alex!" at the sound.

Of course, she knew it couldn't actually be Alex. It never had been before. Still, when she grabbed up the phone, she did take a moment to check the display before she answered.

She gasped and dropped the phone as if it burned her. It was him!

Impossible. But it was. It was really, really him. Alex. Calling her. At long last…

With a cry, she grabbed up the phone again and started to answer—and stopped herself just in time.

No, she would *not* answer. She had left him. She was no longer sitting there, twiddling her thumbs at the Prince's Palace, waiting for him to return. There was nothing to talk about.

Or if there was, he would have to do a lot more than finally pick up the phone to make it happen.

She dropped the phone again and put her hands over her ears and waited for "Dancing Queen" to stop. When it did, she carefully set the phone back on the nightstand and picked up her book again.

A few seconds later, her voice mail chimed.

She tried, oh, she really did, to ignore it. To simply continue reading her very excellent romance and forget all about whatever message he might have condescended to leave her.

But it was impossible. In the end, she tossed the e-reader down and grabbed the phone again.

The phone shook in her hands as she dialed voice mail. And then, there it was.

His voice in her ear after all these endless, awful weeks….

"Lili, it's done." He sounded tired, but somehow good. Somehow…satisfied. "I'll be home to you tomorrow. I've missed you." Her throat clutched. He seemed to mean it. He truly did. "I've missed you so much. I didn't call. I know it. I *should* have called. Should have written. Should have… *something*. But I couldn't. I…" The word trailed off. She held her breath. A tear dribbled down her cheek. She swiped it away. But then he only said, "Tomorrow. I'll be with you. *Really* with you. Tomorrow…"

And that was it. The voice mail robot came on with options. She hung up without choosing one.

And then she sat there, staring blindly at the far wall, the tears falling freely now, dripping off her chin, plopping on the coverlet until she couldn't stand it anymore and she dialed voice mail again, just to hear his voice a second time. She listened to his message all the way through. And then she listened to it again. And then another time after that.

What she somehow managed *not* to do was to call him back.

Alex called again in the morning and left another message. "It's midnight here. I fly out first thing in the morning before dawn. What's going on, Lili? I called our apartment. Rufus answered. He said that you'd gone back to Alagonia. He said you left a letter for me. A letter? Lili, are you all right? Why didn't you return my call?"

An hour later, he called again. "I called my father." His voice was flat. "He says you are well. He says… Lili, have you left me? Lili, what in hell is going on?" That was the end of that message.

After that, he didn't call again.

Lili ached with the need to call him back.

But she didn't. She ate her breakfast. She took a long stroll on the palace grounds. She dealt with correspondence. She painted and she read. She had dinner in the state dining room with her father and some of his ministers and their wives. Everyone said how glad they were to have her home again. She smiled and she chatted. When the meal was over, she joined the others in the music room where a famous pianist played compositions by Liszt and Chopin.

She retired at a little after ten, had a long bath and then went to bed.

She did not call her husband.

The next move was his. She was not making that move for him. Calling was not enough. Coming home to Montedoro was not enough.

He would have to come to Alagonia to get her.

And he would have to convince her beyond a shadow of a doubt that he wanted—that he *chose*—to be her true husband and a real father to their child.

Alone in the master bedroom of their apartment in the Prince's Palace, Alex read again the letter that Lili had left for him:

Alexander,

I've been waiting. Thirty-six days since you left me. Eight hundred and sixty-four hours. Fifty-one thousand eight hundred and forty minutes. Three million, one hundred and ten thousand, four hundred seconds.

Yes, I did the math. After all, I've had plenty of time.

Thirty-six days—and not one phone call from you. Not a single letter. Not a postcard. Not an email or a text.

I was angry when you left. Angry and hurt. I understood that you had to go, understood the necessity to make recompense to the family of your lost friend. What I did not understand was why you had to go alone.

But I was willing to accept that you had to do it your way, willing to put aside my anger and my hurt. Willing to wait for you.

Up to a point.

But I have waited too long. I refuse to wait any longer. It has become clear to me that I have waited more than long enough. I have finally come to realize that in this sad little necessary marriage of ours, I have been the one who has constantly put forth the effort, swallowed her pride, reached out her hand, been willing to try and try again.

From all this constant striving to make things work with you, I have learned a hard and painful lesson. A marriage is not made by one but by two. Without your love, without your honest determination to be with me, to be my husband, without your joy in the journey at my side, we have nothing.

I fear that we have nothing, Alex.

I am going home.

Yours,

Liliana

Nothing.

Alex stared at the words. *I fear we have nothing.*

How could she think that? After the island. After…everything.

Didn't she know that she was his heart? His soul? His future? His rock and his solace?

Didn't she understand that he'd left her only so that he could return to her a free man at last?

Apparently, she did not.

He thought about that. For a very long time.

He also thought about how he really should have called her, even though to call her would only have reminded him that he was far away from her and he wasn't going to allow himself to return to her until he'd finished the task he'd set himself.

Yes, all right. He had been wrong, not to call.

And yes, now he thought back, he had to admit that she was the brave one, the strong one, the one who kept trying over and over, while he constantly hurt her and pushed her away and crawled back into the hole of mourning and self-recrimination he had dug for himself.

He supposed he'd become accustomed to her surprising strength, her impressively steadfast determination to make a husband out of him against all odds. He'd come to count on her putting up with him, being patient with him, always giving him another chance.

Had he run out of chances with her?

His heart seemed to shrink in his chest as he realized that he actually might have managed to accomplish what he'd set out to do when he tricked her into marrying him.

She was giving him what he used to think he wanted: a marriage in name only, the two of them leading separate lives.

The next morning, he met with his father privately in his father's palace office. His Serene Highness Evan had once been a successful film actor in America. He was quite handsome, with gray-streaked dark hair and piercing green eyes that missed nothing.

He pulled no punches. He offered Alex a chair and said frankly, "You've hurt your wife. Deeply."

As if he didn't realize that now. "I just need to see her. She won't take my calls."

"None of us blames her for leaving, Alex. For...cutting off communication with you."

Alex wanted to hit something. Instead, he hung his head. "All right. I've been a blind idiot. I understand that now. What do I do...to make things right? To get my wife back?"

"You do love her?"

"Yes. Absolutely. Of course."

"As a man loves the woman to whom he binds his life?"

"Yes. Like that. Just like that."

His father was silent for a moment. Then he drily advised, "You actually have to learn to say the words, Alex."

"Do you think I'm an idiot?" he demanded. His father only regarded him patiently across the inlaid expanse of his mahogany desk. "All right." He couldn't sit still. He rose, paced to the door and then back again. "I'm a bloody idiot. Didn't I already say that? I see that. I fully understand that now."

"So, then. You have yet to tell your wife that you love her."

He dropped to the chair again, braced his hands on the chair arms, glanced left and then right. Finally, he muttered, "At first, I didn't realize what she meant to me. How important she is. And then, after we were stranded on the island, I knew she meant everything. I knew my true feelings. But I felt that I…didn't have the right to speak of love to her until I had made recompense for the past."

"In other words, no, you haven't told her."

"I was going to. As soon as I got home. I swear I was." The words sounded weak, even to him. They sounded like poor excuses.

"It appears you are a little late," his father observed.

"Damn it. I see that. I understand that. But what do I *do*?"

"Well, you must go after her, of course. My guess would be that she's not going to make it easy for you. And then there will be Leo to get through. That should be interesting."

"Leo. My God."

"Yes. Leo will want his chance to toy with you a bit. The way I see it, Alex, you must not only go after her, but you must also not, under any circumstances, give up and go away."

Alex arrived in Alagonia by helicopter at four that afternoon. With him were two of his most capable, skilled men of the CCU.

Apparently, he had been expected. And not in a good way.

His men were detained at the airport.

Alex was taken under armed guard to D'Alagon. He asked to see his wife. He was ignored.

At the palace, he was led in at a side entrance and down stone stairs, two levels belowground to the world-famous dungeon of D'Alagon, built when the palace was first constructed as a fortified castle back in the thirteenth century. Like most dungeons, it was dank and dim with walls of stone.

He was led to a cell, at which point he asked to see King Leo.

The guards only pushed him into the cell and locked the door.

He surveyed the accommodations. Four windowless stone walls, a ledge for a bed, an open hole in the corner—his toilet, he assumed. It was far from luxurious. But as prisons went, it could have been worse. He knew that from personal experience.

What next?

He knew what: waiting. Probably for a very long while. He could do that. He went and sat on the ledge and told himself to be patient.

Sometime later, he was given a bowl of lamb stew and a cup of water, both pushed through a compartment in the cell door. He ate the stew and drank the water.

And he waited some more. In time, he slept. They'd left him his watch, so he knew it was after four in the morning when he woke.

Eventually, there was breakfast—lukewarm cooked cereal and watery tea. He pondered his thoroughly annoying father-in-law for a time. And he thought of how very much he loved his wife.

Finally, at a little after ten in the morning, they came for him. They hauled him back upstairs to the throne room, where Leo sat alone wearing an Armani suit, his crown and an excessively gleeful expression.

"Your Majesty." Alex bowed as best he could, with a guard holding either arm.

"You need a shave." Leo's smug smile widened.

"And a bath," Alex agreed.

A frown formed between the king's well-trimmed brows. "I told her I would have your head on a pike. But she told me no, that wouldn't do." Leo sighed heavily. "So I suppose I shall have to allow you to keep that thick head of yours."

"Thank you, sir. May I see my wife now?"

Leo waved in a bored and leisurely manner. "I'm afraid not. She doesn't want to see you."

He held his temper. And tried again. "Take me to her. Please."

Leo only shrugged. "You don't seem bothered at all by a night in my dungeon."

"Sir, I only want to speak with my wife."

Leo studied his manicure. "Seriously, Alexander, you are no fun at all."

"Sir, I—"

"She refuses to see you."

"If you would only—"

"No, my boy. It's no good. She will not see you. My men will return you to the airport, after which you and your men will depart Alagonia, never to return. Am I clear?"

Alex considered. What was arguing or disagreeing with Leo going to get him? Nothing. "Very clear, sir."

"I'm sorry it's all worked out so poorly."

You don't seem very sorry. "Yes, sir. I accept your...condolences."

"Go home, Alexander."

"Goodbye, sir."

Leo gestured grandly to the guards. "Take him away."

* * *

An hour later, he and his men lifted off from San Ferdinand. They flew west, out over the open sea. And then, once they were well clear of the southwestern port of Salvia, they circled back, still over water, only approaching land again when they could come in from the north.

They found a wide, dusty field dotted with olive trees several kilometers from the palace. Placid Alagonian sheep regarded them solemnly from a distance as the helicopter touched down.

Still wearing the lightweight designer suit he'd donned the day before in Montedoro, Alex got off alone. He carried a backpack with a change of clothes, a series of scale drawings of D'Alagon, some water, food bars, a computer memory stick and an iPhone.

He stood in the shade of an olive tree and watched the helicopter carrying his men rise and wheel away. Then, swiftly, he took cargo pants, a plain black T-shirt, cotton socks and sturdy shoes from the pack. He changed. He left the wrinkled suit where it fell, beneath the tree, and he set out. The time was one-fifteen in the afternoon.

It was 40 kilometers to D'Alagon. He was capable of keeping a steady, brisk pace of 6.4 kilometers per hour. If all went well, he would arrive at the palace in under seven hours. He would get there a lot faster if he caught a ride. But he'd already decided against that, against getting into a vehicle with a stranger.

He would walk it, and keep an eye out to duck for cover if he spotted anyone too official-looking. The real challenge would be getting in and getting to Lili after he reached her father's palace.

Lili wanted to scream.
He had *left*.

Her father had thrown him in the dungeon overnight and then sent him away.

And Alex had gone.

Given up.

Never mind screaming. Lili wanted to break down and cry. She'd pushed him too far. She'd asked too much of him.

She never should have allowed Papa to put him in that cell. After all he had suffered, all that he had been through in Afghanistan, it had probably caused some terrible flashback, a bad bout of post-traumatic stress. It had probably damaged him immeasurably all over again.

And it was all her fault. She should have picked up the phone that first time he called, should have forgiven the hurt he'd caused her. Should have let bygones be bygones and...

She sank to the edge of her bed, shaking her head.

Really, she didn't know what she *should* have done. It had seemed like the right thing, the *important* thing, to finally draw the line on him, to make him see that he really did have to meet her halfway.

But now, now that he had honestly tried to reach her and she had refused repeatedly to speak with him, had rebuffed him soundly several times...well, now, she just felt that she had pushed this object lesson way too far.

She picked up her cell phone and started to call him.

And then, well, somehow, she just couldn't. Maybe tomorrow. Or the next day.

She knew now that she was going to have to be the one to make the effort, mend the breach.

It was all just too discouraging, all just so very sad.

The clock by the bed said it was after five. She would have a tray sent up. She would read romances all night long and try to lift her spirits, try not to think of poor Alex, of the damage done to him—by thugs and kidnappers.

And by his own wife.

* * *

It was a warm night. Balmy.

At nine, Lili took a long bath. Still feeling sad and lonely and out of sorts, she put on her favorite large, green, faded Ariel the Mermaid T-shirt, opened the windows and the door to the terrace to let the breeze in and climbed into bed.

She picked up her e-reader and began to read.

It was a love scene. A well-written one, too. She tried to get lost in it, but somehow, the passionate ecstasy of the lovers only made her feel more alone. She missed Alex.

She missed him terribly.

It was enough. Too much. She was calling him. She was putting an end to this awfulness now—if only he would speak to her....

No. Enough. She would try. She would make the effort. If he refused to speak with her, she would find another way to reach him.

She grabbed her cell phone and started to dial.

That was when she heard the strange scrabbling noises coming from beyond the terrace doors.

She frowned. Some animal?

Impossible.

It was several stories down to the ground. No animal could possibly have climbed...

A shadow. A...a *man*. There was a man on the terrace. Fear clawed at the back of her throat, kicked her heart into racing mode.

She dropped the phone and jumped from the bed, glancing frantically about for something to use as a weapon.

And then Alex appeared in the open doorway.

Chapter Fifteen

Lili gaped. "Alex?" she got out on a husk of sound.

He stepped into the room with her.

Real.

He was real. He was real and he was here with her. Now.

"Oh, my dear, sweet Lord," she whispered. "Oh, Alex…"

He looked at her as though he never wanted to look away. And then he said, "I'll have to talk to your father. His security is not what it should be."

Tears filled her eyes. "Oh, Alex…"

He shrugged off a backpack, tossed it onto a chair. "Lili. God. Lili." And then he came to her. She gasped again, put her hand to her mouth.

Real. He was dusty, sweaty and he looked tired. But he was also so very wonderfully, perfectly real.

She reached for him. He caught her hand, kissed it so tenderly. Heat sizzled up her arm just from that light, cherishing contact.

And then he sank to one knee in front of her.

She gasped again. "Oh, Alex. No. Don't…"

He gazed up at her, eyes all warm amber light. He said, "Forgive me, Lili. I love you, Lili. Come back to me, Lili. I've screwed things up, I know it. I'm not worthy of you, but I do love you. You're my light, my shining star. You gave me back my life. You gave me everything. I should have said it, said I love you, before I left for America. But I had some idea that I had to pay all my debts to the past before I could claim you, claim our future."

"Oh, Alex…"

"And then, I didn't call. That was very stupid."

"Oh, yes," she answered tenderly, her heart so full that it seemed too big for her chest. "It was. Stupid and wrong. You really should have called."

"I couldn't bear to. I missed you so. If I'd heard your voice…I don't know, I just couldn't."

"All right. I can accept that. In the future, however…"

"Yes, I will call. *If* I ever leave you again. I don't think that I could."

She laughed then. "Of course, you could. And you will." She sniffled, brushed a tear from her eye. "But when you do, you have to call. Communication does matter in a marriage."

"I know. You're right. I see that now."

"Alex…"

"Yes. Absolutely. Anything. Name it."

She tugged on his hand. "You can get up now."

"Not yet. Not until you say you'll come back to me."

"Of course, I'll come back to you."

"Say it again."

"Alex, I love you. Yes, I'll come back to you."

He did rise then. And he swept her into those big, strong arms and he kissed her long and thoroughly.

Then she pulled him down to sit on the bed beside her

and she leaned her head on his shoulder. "I can't believe you scaled the palace wall. Are you insane? You might have fallen."

"Shh," he said. He stroked her hair. It felt so good. She had missed that, the simple feel of his hand stroking her hair.

"Are you hungry?"

"Shh…" He put his hand on her belly. "Fuller. He's growing."

"She'll start kicking soon—and I have to know. So much. Everything. That's what happens when you don't call. There's so much to catch up on…."

He chuckled and gave in. "Ask, then."

"Did you meet with them—Devon's parents, his brothers and sisters?"

"I did. His father was angry at first, wouldn't speak with me. But eventually, with his mother's help, he gave in. We talked. It was…good. Not easy, but good. Then there were Dev's brothers and sisters. One brother was happy to talk to me. The others were unwilling. But I kept at it. In time, I… got through, I guess you could say."

"You made financial arrangements?"

"Yes, college funds. Trusts. I know, it's only money, but…"

"We do what we can."

"Well said." And he kissed her again. And then again.

And then both of them forgot for a time about talking.

It was so sweet, their reunion. Sweet and hot and wonderful.

Afterward, she drew a bath for him. And then joined him in it.

She lay back against his broad, warm chest and dared to suggest, "It would make quite a book, don't you think? The story of your capture and imprisonment, of how you went to America and met Devon's family…"

He shook his head, pressed his lips against her hair. "I don't think so. I lived it. It was enough. At least not now. Not for a good long while."

"So eventually you do want to write again?"

"I *have* been writing."

She took his hand, placed it on her belly. It felt so good there. "Oh, Alex, that's wonderful."

He cradled her breast, kissed the side of her neck. "I started a whole new story, something completely different. I found it took my mind off missing you so much, off the tensions with Dev's family. It's an adventure story. Two star-crossed lovers, marooned on a Mediterranean island..."

Water sloshed over the tub rim as she turned around to lie against him, face-to-face. "You're teasing me. You would never write a story like that. Why, that's almost...a romance."

"Lili, my love." He kissed the tip of her nose. "It *is* a romance. I brought a copy with me, of what I have so far. On a memory stick."

She blinked. "Alex, are you serious?"

"Later, you can read it, see what you think. I mean, if you would like to take a look..."

"Alex, I would *love* to read whatever you've written, especially a romance. But...oh, Alex. What has gotten into you?"

"I think you know." He said it so tenderly. And then, "I love you, Lili."

"And I love you, Alex."

"We're a family now." He said it so proudly.

She whispered, "Forever, Alex."

"Yes." His amber gaze met hers, unwavering. "That's it. That's exactly it, what I've been longing for. You and me, Lili. Together. For the rest of our lives."

Epilogue

"We miss you," Lili said.

Arabella clutched the phone a little tighter and stared at the cornucopia decoration that Charlotte, her aide and companion, had arranged on the breakfast room table. It was the day before Thanksgiving.

But Belle was having a hard time feeling thankful. She was at her dear friend Anne's house in the States, in Raleigh, North Carolina. Anne was very ill and not expected to last out the week.

At home in Montedoro, they would all be looking forward to the Thanksgiving feast. At home in Montedoro at the Prince's Palace where Belle had grown up, they'd always celebrated the American holiday. Belle's father, the prince consort, had been born in America on a ranch called Bravo Ridge. The ranch was in the state of Texas, not far from the city of San Antonio.

Her father's childhood had not been a happy one. He'd told them the stories of his lonely boyhood. He had six brothers, but he'd never felt close to any of them. His father, James Bravo, had been an angry, bitter, violent man. And his mother, Elizabeth, was strange and distant, her eyes always sad and far away. As a boy, Belle's father had dreamed of a happier future, of the family he would make when he became a man, a family where they had joyful Christmases. And real Thanksgivings.

Her father had that family now, a family that gratefully celebrated Thanksgiving.

"Belle?" Lili asked. "Are you there?"

"I'm here, Lili," she said into the phone. "Sorry. Feeling a little down, I guess."

"I keep praying."

"Hoping for a miracle, hmm?"

"Oh, Belle, yes. A miracle. Absolutely."

Dear Lili. Always looking on the bright side. Belle asked, "How are *you* feeling?"

"Fat. Very fat." Lili was having twins. A boy and a girl.

Belle chuckled. They'd had a rough time of it at the first, Lili and Alex. But they had made it through. "I'm so glad, so happy for you. And for Alex."

Lili agreed. "Yes, so am I. So very glad."

"You deserve your happiness, Lili. You both do. Happy Thanksgiving."

"Thank you." Lili didn't say it back to her. Belle was grateful for that. It wasn't a happy Thanksgiving for her this year. There was no way that it could be. "How's the little one, Benjamin?" Lili asked.

Anne's son was just eighteen months old. "Adorable. Perfect. And napping at the moment."

"Give him extra kisses for me."

Belle smiled at the thought. "I will. I promise."

They chatted for a while longer and then they said goodbye.

Belle set down the phone and felt in her pocket. The envelope was there, a reminder of encroaching shadows. A talisman in a way.

Anne had pressed it into her hand just yesterday. "Read it after I'm gone," she had said.

Belle closed her fingers around the envelope and pulled it out of her pocket. Just a plain white envelope with her name written in Anne's forward-slanting hand across the front. It was already looking a bit worn and wrinkled. Somehow, Belle couldn't stop herself from touching it, from hauling it out and holding it up to the light, wondering what was on the sheet of paper inside, before stuffing it back in her pocket again.

Read it after I'm gone....

Five little words. Three of them terrible: *after I'm gone....*

Charlotte stuck her head in from the hall, her eyes ringed with shadows, her face drawn. Belle knew that her own face, though younger, bore the same lines of weariness. "She's asking for you."

Belle eased the envelope back into her pocket and straightened her sagging shoulders. She put on a smile. "I'm coming." She went down the hall to her friend's bedroom, the letter crackling against her pocket as she walked.

Read it after I'm gone....

A princess by birth, but a nurse by profession, Belle longed for a miracle, but she knew the hard truth.

It would not be long now.

* * * * *

Watch for Belle's story,
THE RANCHER'S CHRISTMAS PRINCESS,
coming in December 2012,
only from Harlequin Special Edition.

COMING NEXT MONTH from Harlequin
Special Edition®
AVAILABLE JUNE 19, 2012

#2197 THE LAST SINGLE MAVERICK
Montana Mavericks: Back in the Saddle
Christine Rimmer
Steadfastly single cowboy Jason Traub asks Jocelyn Bennings to accompany him to his family reunion to avoid any blind dates his family has planned for him. Little does he know that she's a runaway bride—and that he's about to lose his heart to her!

#2198 THE PRINCESS AND THE OUTLAW
Royal Babies
Leanne Banks
Princess Pippa Devereaux has never defied her family except when it comes to Nic Lafitte. But their feuding families won't be enough to keep these star-crossed lovers apart.

#2199 HIS TEXAS BABY
Men of the West
Stella Bagwell
The relationship of rival horse breeders Kitty Cartwright and Liam Donovan takes a whole new turn when an unplanned pregnancy leads to an unplanned romance.

#2200 A MARRIAGE WORTH FIGHTING FOR
McKinley Medics
Lilian Darcy
The last thing Alicia McKinley expects when she leaves her husband, MJ, is for him to put up a fight for their marriage. What surprises her even more is that she starts falling back in love with him.

#2201 THE CEO'S UNEXPECTED PROPOSAL
Reunion Brides
Karen Rose Smith
High school crushes Dawson Barrett and Mikala Conti are reunited when Dawson asks her to help his traumatized son recover from an accident. When sparks fly and a baby on the way complicates things even more, can this couple make it work?

#2202 LITTLE MATCHMAKERS
Jennifer Greene
Being a single parent is hard, but Garnet Cottrell and Tucker MacKinnon have come up with a "kid-swapping" plan to help give their boys a more well-rounded upbringing. But unbeknownst to their parents the boys have a matchmaking plan of their own.

You can find more information on upcoming Harlequin® titles, free excerpts and more at www.HarlequinInsideRomance.com.

HSECNM0612

REQUEST YOUR FREE BOOKS!
2 FREE NOVELS PLUS 2 FREE GIFTS!

♦ Harlequin®

SPECIAL EDITION

Life, Love & Family

YES! Please send me 2 FREE Harlequin® Special Edition novels and my 2 FREE gifts (gifts are worth about $10). After receiving them, if I don't wish to receive any more books, I can return the shipping statement marked "cancel." If I don't cancel, I will receive 6 brand-new novels every month and be billed just $4.49 per book in the U.S. or $5.24 per book in Canada. That's a saving of at least 14% off the cover price! It's quite a bargain! Shipping and handling is just 50¢ per book in the U.S. and 75¢ per book in Canada.* I understand that accepting the 2 free books and gifts places me under no obligation to buy anything. I can always return a shipment and cancel at any time. Even if I never buy another book, the two free books and gifts are mine to keep forever.

235/335 HDN FEGF

Name	
	(PLEASE PRINT)
Address	Apt. #
City	State/Prov.	Zip/Postal Code

Signature (if under 18, a parent or guardian must sign)

Mail to the **Reader Service:**
IN U.S.A.: P.O. Box 1867, Buffalo, NY 14240-1867
IN CANADA: P.O. Box 609, Fort Erie, Ontario L2A 5X3

Not valid for current subscribers to Harlequin Special Edition books.

Want to try two free books from another line?
Call 1-800-873-8635 or visit www.ReaderService.com.

* Terms and prices subject to change without notice. Prices do not include applicable taxes. Sales tax applicable in N.Y. Canadian residents will be charged applicable taxes. Offer not valid in Quebec. This offer is limited to one order per household. All orders subject to credit approval. Credit or debit balances in a customer's account(s) may be offset by any other outstanding balance owed by or to the customer. Please allow 4 to 6 weeks for delivery. Offer available while quantities last.

Your Privacy—The Reader Service is committed to protecting your privacy. Our Privacy Policy is available online at www.ReaderService.com or upon request from the Reader Service.

We make a portion of our mailing list available to reputable third parties that offer products we believe may interest you. If you prefer that we not exchange your name with third parties, or if you wish to clarify or modify your communication preferences, please visit us at www.ReaderService.com/consumerschoice or write to us at Reader Service Preference Service, P.O. Box 9062, Buffalo, NY 14269. Include your complete name and address.

HSE11B

The Bowman siblings have avoided Christmas ever since a family tragedy took the lives of their parents during the holiday years ago. But twins Trace and Taft Bowman have gotten past their grief, courtesy of the new women in their lives. Is it sister Caidy's turn to find love—perhaps with the new veterinarian in town?

Read on for an excerpt from
A COLD CREEK NOEL by USA TODAY bestselling author RaeAnne Thayne, next in her ongoing series THE COWBOYS OF COLD CREEK

***

"For what it's worth, I think the guys around here are crazy. Even if you did grow up with them."

He might have left things at that, safe and uncomplicated, except his eyes suddenly shifted to her mouth and he didn't miss the flare of heat in her gaze. He swore under his breath, already regretting what he seemed to have no power to resist, and then he reached for her.

As his mouth settled over hers, warm and firm and tasting of cocoa, Caidy couldn't quite believe this was happening.

She was being kissed by the sexy new veterinarian, just a day after thinking him rude and abrasive. For a long moment she was shocked into immobility, then heat began to seep through her frozen stupor. Oh. Oh, yes!

How long had it been since she had enjoyed a kiss and wanted more? She was astounded to realize she couldn't really remember. As his lips played over hers, she shifted her neck slightly for a better angle. Her insides seemed to give a collective shiver. Mmm. This was exactly what two people ought to be doing at 3:00 a.m. on a cold December day.

He made a low sound in his throat that danced down her spine, and she felt the hard strength of his arms slide around her, pulling her closer. In this moment, nothing else seemed to matter but Ben Caldwell and the wondrous sensations fluttering through her.

Still, this was crazy. Some tiny voice of self-preservation seemed to whisper through her. What was she doing? She had no business kissing someone she barely knew and wasn't even sure she liked yet.

Though it took every last ounce of strength, she managed to slide away from all that delicious heat and move a few inches away from him, trying desperately to catch her breath.

The distance she created between them seemed to drag Ben back to his senses. He stared at her, his eyes looking as dazed as she felt. "That was wrong. I don't know what I was thinking. Your dog is a patient and…I shouldn't have…"

She might have been offended by the dismay in his voice if not for the arousal in his eyes. But his hair was a little rumpled and he had the evening shadow of a beard and all she could think was *yum*.

***

Can Caidy and Ben put their collective pasts behind them and find a brilliant future together?

Find out in A COLD CREEK NOEL, coming in December 2012 from Harlequin Special Edition. And coming in 2013, also from Harlequin Special Edition, look for Ridge's story….

A brand-new Westmoreland novel from *New York Times* bestselling author

BRENDA JACKSON

Riley Westmoreland never mixes business with pleasure—until he meets his company's gorgeous new party planner. But when he gets Alpha Blake into bed, he realizes one night will never be enough. That's when her past threatens to end their affair. So Riley does what any Westmoreland male would do...he lets the fun begin.

ONE WINTER'S NIGHT

"Jackson's characters are...hot enough to burn the pages."
—*RT Book Reviews* on *Westmoreland's Way*

Available from Harlequin® Desire December 2012!

HARLEQUIN *Presents*®

When legacy commands, these Greek royals must obey!

Discover a page-turning new Harlequin Presents®
duet from *USA TODAY* bestselling author

Maisey Yates

A ROYAL WORLD APART

Desperate to escape an arranged marriage, Princess
Evangelina has tried every trick in her little black book
to dodge her security guards. But where everyone else
has failed, will her new bodyguard bend her to his
will…and steal her heart?

Available November 13, 2012.

AT HIS MAJESTY'S REQUEST

Prince Stavros Drakos rules his country like his
business—with a will of iron! And when duty demands
an heir, this resolute bachelor will turn his sole
focus to the task….

But will he finally have met his match in a world-
renowned matchmaker?

**Coming December 18, 2012,
wherever books are sold.**

Harlequin® *Desire*

ALWAYS POWERFUL, PASSIONATE AND PROVOCATIVE.

**DON'T MISS THE SEDUCTIVE CONCLUSION
TO THE MINISERIES**

THE HIGHEST BIDDER

WITH FAN-FAVORITE AUTHOR

BARBARA DUNLOP

Prince Raif Khouri believes that Waverly's
high-end-auction-house executive Ann Richardson
is responsible for the theft of his valuable antique Gold
Heart statue, rumored to be a good luck charm to his
family. The only way Raif can keep an eye on her—
and get the truth from her—is by kidnapping Ann and
taking her to his kingdom. But soon Raif finds himself
the prisoner as Ann tempts him like no one else.

A GOLDEN BETRAYAL

Available December 2012 from Harlequin® Desire.

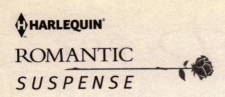

Get your heart racing this holiday season with double the pulse-pounding action.

Christmas Confidential

Featuring

Holiday Protector by **Marilyn Pappano**

Miri Duncan doesn't care that it's almost Christmas. She's got bigger worries on her mind. But surviving the trip to Georgia from Texas is going to be her biggest challenge. Days in a car with the man who broke her heart and helped send her to prison—private investigator Dean Montgomery.

A Chance Reunion by **Linda Conrad**

When the husband Elana Novak left behind five years ago shows up in her new California home she knows danger is coming her way. To protect the man she is quickly falling for Elana must convince private investigator Gage Chance that she is a different person. But Gage isn't about to let her walk away…even with the bad guys right on their heels.

Available December 2012 wherever books are sold!

www.Harlequin.com

HRS27801